MW01596119

BOOKS
AS DRINKING BUDDIES

A Book of Re-Readings

Select Books by Gary Soto

POETRY
Downtime, 2023
The Elements of San Joaquin (expanded and revised), 2018
Meatballs for the People: Proverbs to Chew On, 2017
You Kiss by th' Book: New Poems from Shakespeare's Line, 2016
Sudden Loss of Dignity, 2013
Human Nature, 2010
A Simple Plan, 2007
One Kind of Faith, 2003
A Natural Man, 1999
Junior College, 1997
New and Selected Poems, 1995
Home Course in Religion, 1991
Who Will Know Us?, 1990
Black Hair, 1985
Where Sparrows Work Hard, 1981
The Tale of Sunlight, 1978
The Elements of San Joaquin, 1977

PROSE
Sit Still! A Poet's Need to See and Do Everything, 2020
F. Pérez Lopez's El Mexicano, 2018
Why I Don't Write Children's Literature, 2015
What Poets Are Like, 2013
Amnesia in a Republican County, 2003
Poetry Lover, 2001
Nickel and Dime, 2000
The Effects of Knut Hamsun on a Fresno Boy, 2000
Jesse, 1994
A Summer Life, 1990
Small Faces, 1986
Living Up the Street, 1985

BOOKS
AS DRINKING BUDDIES

A Book of Re-Readings

GARY SOTO

 LIMBERLOST PRESS

Boise, Idaho
2026

Acknowledgments

The pieces in the Endnotes first appeared in *The Guardian* (London), *Readers Digest*, and *The Rod Stewart Fan Club*. Chapters on re-reading books by Jonas Jonasson, Nick Hornby, and Francois Boucher, and T.S. Eliot first appeared in *The Limberlost Review: A Literary Journal of the Mountain West, 2025*.

The moral right of the influencer to publish this silliness has been asserted. He may be reached by calling his landline at (510) 845-4718. The MacArthur Foundation may reach him by looking up his street address at www.garysoto.com. He's in his comfy armchair this very moment.

The influencer acknowledges his first readers, Carolyn Soto and Peter Fong. Rick and Rosemary Ardinger spilled ink for the cause. Meggan Laxalt Mackey conjured up a stellar design.

Published by ⟡ LIMBERLOST PRESS

Cover photos: Carolyn Sadako Oda

Book design and photo art: Meggan Laxalt Mackey,
Studio M Publications & Design

For a complete catalog, please visit the Limberlost Press website:
www.limberlostpress.com

Library of Congress Cataloging-in-Publication Data:
 Soto, Gary. *Books as Drinking Buddies: A Book of Re-Readings*
 ISBN 979-8-2954-8346-2
 All rights reserved
 First edition, April 2026
 Printed in the United States of America

For Carolyn

With needle and thread,
she mends my mistakes.

TABLE OF CONTENTS

PREFACE
Gary Soto, XV

RE-READINGS

ENDNOTES

Beer is proof that Gods loves us and wants us to be happy.

—Benjamin Franklin

PREFACE

WHILE GIVING A TALK AT A HIGH SCHOOL IN NAPA,
California, a student asked, "Mr. Soto, are you an influencer?"
Influencer? I wondered as I cast my eyes to the floor. There was that
word again—*influencer*. Was I being left behind? I told the youth
to decide for himself once the school day was over. I continued
with a mildly entertaining story about a seagull that once flew
away with my sweater.

The school bell rang, the chairs were noisily pushed aside,
and phones appeared from the long sleeves of hoodies. The teacher thanked me, and I thanked her. I waved to the student who had
asked if I was an influencer, asking him to follow me to my car.
The Buick Century was dull gray and dented in several places. The
tires were worn, the grill crushed, just slightly. The student looked
from the car to the visiting author and back to the car. *No, he's not
an influencer,* I read in his face. The student observed, "You parked
under a tree. You got bird poop on the windshield."

The student went away, the day as well. But I kept brooding
over the word *influencer,* and how an older generation of poets
and writers missed their chances to grab the world's attention.
True, a few are on Instagram and TikTok, and some are making
noise on X. But for us in our seventies, we ignore social media.
We embrace books: commercial and university press, small-press
and limited-edition beauties, and self-published staple jobs done
at copy centers. Influencers revel in talk—the louder the better,
it seems. And the farther from the truth, the better. Outrageous
facts and figures rule. Nastiness owns the room. Clichés are hurled
like horseshoes.

Poets and writers, we have feet of clay. *Why is that? Why aren't
we loud? We could build audiences, correct?* Most of us are frustrated
by the absence of attention. When a reader tells us, "I liked your

last book," however, we wag our metaphorical tails. It feels good to be loved. But we fail to sprint into action.

I'm a poet, age seventy-three, momentary influencer with a trickster inside him. I've worked in all genres. This includes poetry and essays, adult fiction, plays, children's literature, opera, filmscripts, films themselves, and now this, a collection of book reviews that are often more about me than the books themselves. You're not supposed to learn from any of this or believe wholly in my critical reports. You're meant to have fun, with a proper drink in your paw. There are serious and frivolous titles in my reviews—you ponder which is which. I have enjoyed all of them from our household's "comfy armchair."

From this perch, I drink, and I flirt with my drink—you'll see. My wife, a clothes designer, is usually present, a foil to the outrageous things I say. She's on Instagram and I'm on Super Mario Brothers from Atari. Frustrated by my fossilized approach to self-promotion, she has told me repeatedly what I'm supposed to do, social media, I mean. Our biggest argument involves the geography of the Easter Islands.

We've been married fifty years. You'll see.

RE-READINGS

THE HUNDRED-YEAR-OLD MAN WHO CLIMBED OUT OF THE WINDOW AND DISAPPEARED

By Jonas Jonasson

HERE, ON THIS PAGE, I'M NOT A BOOK REVIEWER but an *influencer*, a word that recently parted the wiry hairs around my ears and entered my gray matter. I get it now: influencers are people who would like us to think how they think. *Podcast* is another such word. Podcast means you are expected to listen to people who are not in the room that you're in, but faraway, like Idaho or Montana, where trucks outnumber people. Podcasts involve headsets and electronics, I think, and time zones, I also think. For this sort of activity, no license from the FCC is needed to talk stupid.

Let me take up your time by highlighting a novel that involves, in part, time—or the lack of it. I refer to Jonas Jonasson's *The Hundred-Year-Old Man Who Climbed Out of the Window and Disappeared*. Even if I influence you, the book doesn't need me. This 2012 bestseller was first published in Sweden and then, with cheerful clamor, traveled worldwide. The novel sold 11 million copies, which allowed the author to purchase a home on the Swedish island of Gotland and has been translated into every major language. (But hold your Christian horses, readers. Let's think about this. Isn't every language a major language if you're the one speaking it?)

The novel features our eccentric hero Allan Karlsson, who's locked in a state-run nursing home, a birthday boy who sours at the thought of a party among other residents befuddled by age. Karlsson will not have any of it. He is stubborn, so stubborn, and sober to boot: the head nurse keeps confiscating his bottles of vodka. Without a proper drink, life is grim, nearly impossible, a pitiful existence. But he's wily and cagey, we quickly learn, with a verifiable history of bravery. He carries out his escape by slipping out a window and into a flower bed, smashing a few precious petunias in the process. He looks about. *Should I go left or right?* he wonders. Then he eyes his feet: he's wearing a pair of "pee slippers." Like, what? Did you read that correctly? Pee slippers? Is it true that men his age—or as young as seventy-three—can't pee farther than their slippers when they're standing at the bowl? How can this be, when most teens can pee the length of a football field?

Forgive this influencer. I'm neither the late Hugh Kenner nor Harold Bloom nor even an assistant professor at a state college in the Midwest. The literary significance of pee slippers must be small, so why bring it up? I'll drop it now—and for good.

To continue: Karlsson is of sound mind and not done with life. True, he is a hundred on the day of his escape and putters about with a bent back. He's old, certifiably old. No wash-cloth has yet been patented that could wipe away the wrinkles on his Nordic face. Yet he's alive, not like his amigo, Henning Algotsson, who made a career-changing decision by dying at age thirty-nine. Is Algotsson important in this escapade? Not really. But if you escape from a window of a nursing home, travel down a lane and, within a hundred yards, find yourself in a churchyard cemetery where your friend is buried, then, yes, maybe it is worthy of comment. Still, like the pee slippers, I'm done with Henning Algotsson.

Perhaps it's time for me to ramp up my critical appreciation of this 384-page novel.

It's totally good.

But is this a novel about aches and pains? Memory loss? Hair loss? The worm of an old man's sexual organ that was once the snake of desire? Not in the least. It's an adventure, which is estab-lished on page 5 when Karlsson, already on the run, purchases a bus ticket that departs (he looks up at the station's clock) in three minutes, the exact amount of time it would have taken him to blow out a hundred candles on his cake back at the nursing home. And the reader will recognize the dramatic tension when a young gangster (they're in Sweden too) asks our hero to guard his roller-bag suitcase while he goes and takes a "dump," the author's word, not mine. Our hero blinks at the suitcase and considers the moment as his bus honks its horn for latecomers to giddy-up and get their asses on board. He rises from a bench, takes the roller-bag suitcase, and boards the bus, which pulls away from the curb before the gangster emerges from the john, zipping up.

Young Bad Guy without a suitcase, steaming mad, mutters: "You're a dead man, you old bastard. Once I've found you."

This threat occurs on page 9, with justifiable anger. I mean, come on, what has the world come to when you can't trust an old geezer?

A few pages later, Young Bad Guy kidnaps a bus driver, along with the bus, and tracks down Karlsson in a rural town of no importance where, an hour earlier, our hero, still trudging in his pee slippers, encountered a loner named Julius Jonsson. And how deep is this new character's loneliness? He hadn't spoken to a soul in several years until Karlsson, in desperation, asked for help. It was near sunset, I believe, when surely in Sweden a man's nuts have a habit of crawling into his body for warmth. There's a remedy, though, when one is shivering from the cold: vodka, lots of that clear stuff. Jonsson and Karlsson become friends over a proper drink, then lifelong buds after six shots.

But unbeknownst to the new friends, Young Bad Guy has located Karlsson, who unwisely has pulled the roller-bag suitcase over gravel, leaving tracks to follow. Young Bad Guy giggles to himself; he's found the old bastard (again the author's word, not mine). Young Bad Guy boldly enters the building while Karlsson is taking a leak in a closet-like toilet just off the kitchen. Karlsson stalls for a second when he hears a commotion. He zips up and returns to the kitchen, where he discovers Young Bad Guy twisting Julius Jonsson's ears. Brave Karlsson will not have any of that. He looks about for a suitable weapon. His choices: a crowbar, a wooden plank, insect spray, or rat poison He decides on the plank. Raising it like a crucifix, he brings it down against the forehead of Young Bad Guy, who falls and clips his gourd on the edge of the kitchen table.

No blood, no visible wound. Do stars rotate inside his thick skull? It's anyone's guess.

The unconscious villain is heaved like a sack of potatoes into the freezer where elk meat is stored, possibly along with the antlers that larger Swedes use as toothpicks. He wakes up a few minutes later and groggily bangs on the door. Karlsson and Jonsson wave off his threats, which are muffled by the freezer's noisy motor. They sit down to dessert, then more drinks—lots of drinks, I imagine, because they forget about Young Bad Guy. The next morning, Jonsson opens the freezer to fetch a slab of bacon and—oops, his bad! The young man, hugging himself, wears a coat of frost. He is dead as the bacon, dead as the elk.

In Chapter 4, titled "1905-1929," we glimpse the backstory of Karlsson's life, which began on May 2, 1905, he the son of a radical woman who marched in May Day parades and hollered to the heavens for an eight-hour workday. His father was a railroad worker, an open-minded man who believed, for instance, in contraceptives. Every week, he dutifully handed his wages over to his wife. The chapter provides lovely details and some comforting moments. I should enlarge upon them, but as an influencer I recognize the brief attention span of my followers. So, let's return to the present—2005, the year of our narrative—and Julius Jonsson licking the spoon he has previously used for supper. He pries open the suitcase. Holy shit! A treasure! Bundles of 500-crown notes, to the tune of 37 million. Neither of the men whistle at that sum. Me, I would have sung like a bird!

Mucho dinero!

There's never a dull moment in the novel. You like elephants? They're in there, as are Chairman Mao, President Truman, Stalin, Kim Il-sung, Einstein, Einstein's brother, landlocked dictators, a Russian czar, mysterious lovelies, rivers that sweep away all guilt, a platoon or two of the French Foreign Legion, along with a few seemingly inflated tales that involve the Spanish Civil War and the Manhattan Project—all with our benign hero padding about in boots, clogs, dress shoes, loafers, and pee slippers.

We love our man. He's an indestructible anti-hero worth rooting for, a survivor who went to war and came back from war. For one week, down with French novels! For two weeks, sneer at Chekhov and Dostoevsky! Tonight, I might throw my chops into a plate of herring, with proper drinks of course. I'll eat by candle-light and, once finished, permit my kitten to lick my fingers. I'm a happy clam.

And, finally, out of courtesy to Swedish men, I will admit that I'm fully aware that you don't use elk antlers as toothpicks. But, *ay, chihuahua*, can you guys drink yourselves beautifully senseless.

SONGBOOK

By Nick Hornby

THERE'S NO REST FOR INFLUENCERS. WE RECOGNIZE our duty to humanity. We're busy herding our followers toward viewpoints that will make them ponder life until the next paycheck. This brings me to Hornby's favorite bands and songs—songs hummed, I imagine, as he cobbled together this delightfully readable book. He confesses in the initial pages that he doesn't listen to either classical or jazz giants. I'm surprised at this exclusion by a lauded British novelist, an Academy Award nominee for screenplays, a commercially successful writer with the freedom to call his own shots during the day.

Still, I shrug at his apparent indifference. Me, I could listen for hours to "The Flower Duet" from *Lakmé* or Dave Brubeck, with a proper drink in my paw. But Bach? I could sit still for maybe twenty minutes. And Pharaoh Sanders? Six minutes of screeching sax should do it.

I skim this book with interest. I scour the names of rock groups that I missed in my own musical upbringing. Let's see, what do we have here . . . a group called the Blockheads? Funny, I thought they were the twins that lived next door to us, who did a little time in juvie, a longer time in a prison, and finally an even longer sentence in a cemetery outside of Fresno. But Hornby thinks highly of this group, and because I think highly of Hornby, I make a mental note to check out the Blockheads. What about a band called Suicide and their song, "Frankie Teardrop"? Hornby describes it as "ten and a half minutes of genuinely terrifying industrial noise, a sort of aural equivalent of *Eraserhead*."

Gee, that sounds like a danceable tune, if your partner is an inflatable doll. Spooky.

In the comfort of my living room, I scratch the top of my itchy skull, where black hair once waved with genius, then flew away when, during a Sunday drive, I rolled down the window of my Buick Century. I scratch my dome, sip my St. Pauli Girl, and blink at the water stain on the ceiling. Now, what is the water stain telling me? Sometimes it resembles an elephant, other times a smiling fawn. My mind, a gray mush, is wandering.

Think, Gary, I tell myself. Get a grip!

I scan the table of contents of this 2002 publication. I become confused. I don't know of any of this music. Who is Nelly Furtado, Mark Mulcahy, Röyksopp, The Avalanches, Soulwax, The Bible, The Chemical Brothers, Ron Sexsmith, O. V. Wright, or Badly Drawn Boy? Patti Smith—oh, I've heard of her. Here Hornby speaks to the almighty heavens about her ditty, "Pissing in the River." This underpaid influencer wonders whether Smith waded into the river to pee or let it roll down her slender legs as she stood on a sandy bank.

Music gives us pleasure and the chance to be somewhere else, perhaps even to be someone with celebrity status. For a few minutes in 1975, I wanted to be Bruce Springsteen, a rocker with immense talent and a bouncy stage presence. I also wanted to be Paul McCartney in 1965, and then, after a costume change, Little Richard, the King and Queen of Rock and Roll. But after the night ended and the fans dispersed, I preferred to return to my regular junior-high status—a nobody.

In *Songbook*, Hornby praises the expected figures like The Beatles, Rod Stewart, Aretha Franklin, and The Supremes, who all recorded catchy tunes. He's a spendthrift with his generosity—he likes lots of music. There are references to Sonny Boy Williamson, Jackson Browne, Smokey Robinson, the brother who did "Let's Get It On," Rufus Wainwright, and the durable Willie Nelson. There is a small moment when he cites a CD called *Reggae for Kids*. Got to start them young: kids grooving in a park, their faces stained with cotton candy.

I'm an influencer who works for nothing. Yet, like you, my followers, I'm also a human with a heart, lungs, and a digestive tract. I raise my head toward the ceiling. I blink, I sip my suds, I wipe my tired eyes and sigh at the meaning of it all. Jesus, that water stain is now a dead ringer for a baby hippo. No, a robot from a Japanese film from the 1950s. I consider my bottle of St. Pauli Girl, drain it, then set it aside, my first of six for the evening.

Van Morrison? He's the rocker of all geriatric rockers. Hornby says *It's Too Late to Stop Now* is "the most enjoyable album, unarguably, so don't even think about arguing" and proposes that a song from the album could be used as the movie credits roll. Now that's high praise—got to locate Van Morrison's music on YouTube and play him loud, with hearing aids in, my equally deaf cat in my lap.

I haven't listened to a lot of the groups and solo acts refer-enced in *Songbook*. Hornby sometimes becomes opinionated, even angry, when the public applauds the inane. He puts his foot down on the sordid 1980 punk rockers. Witty him, he invents a few names for these bands. He would never listen to rockers with names like Thuggy, Breakskull, and PusShit. Girl singers with coiffured hairdos? No. And no to rockers with blood coming out their nostrils. Hornby likes what he likes. Joni Mitchell, for instance, he doesn't quite trust— or at least the album called *Blue*. Maybe it's a guy thing, maybe not. I admit that I never followed Mitchell's music.

I stopped my musical journey about the time I could afford Santana's *Abraxas*—great album, the pride of Chicanos. What? Did you hear right? Yes, your influencer did not bother much with music beyond the early 1970s. I followed some artists, like Fleetwood Mac, and in the 1980s was head-bobbing to George Clinton's "Atomic Dog," plus a song or two by mumbling Bob Dylan. And for a few horny hours in the early 1980s, I had a major crush on Blondie—I just loved her teeth. Every one of her songs was dedicated to me.

But since my personality was starched into place by the late 1960s, I remained musically stuck in that period—or in the period that preceded the Beatles and Stones and Motown.

Examples, please? you ask. OK, readers, I will keep it short. I name Nancy Sinatra—in and out of go-go boots—and Bobbie Gentry with her false eyelashes in place. I loved the Ronettes, the Supremes, Harry Belafonte, Dusty Springfield, Lou Rawls, the Righteous Brothers, Brenda Lee, and hip-shaking Lulu singing "Shout!" The theme song to *Bonanza?* It's right up there.

But my favorite, the one song that did it to me, came out about the same time that my blockhead neighbors first bunked down in juvie. I gulp here and lift my eyes back to the water stain on the ceiling, which suddenly resembles my cat's pawprints. *How in the world,* I wonder, *how did our furry gentleman manage to walk on the ceiling?*

OK, I'm stalling. But now I'm ready to fess up. I—influencer to an audience in several western states, including Idaho and Montana—admit that my favorite song from the 1960s is "Sukiyaki" by Kyu Sakamoto.

A period of silence is due here. Go ahead and scratch your own depleted scalp, adjust your bra strap if you must. Get up and go to the fridge for another icy brew.

I repeat, "Sukiyaki" by Kyu Sakamoto.

More silence, with added eye blinking. Has that mushy brain finally drained into my digestive tract? Should I hurry to the toilet?

Let me explain. "Sukiyaki," also called "Ue o Muite Aruko" ("I Look Up When I Walk"), was a massive tsunami hit in Japan, with millions of red vinyl copies sold in 1961. The song next traveled to Australia and England and finally, in 1963, to the United States. It became a sensation in the Japanese American community in my hometown of Fresno, a song embraced because of its message—walk with your head up.

And why? If you know our nation's history, many Japanese Americans (along with a few confused Peruvian Japanese who were arrested for no reason and ferried to our country) were put into concentration camps during World War II. After President

Franklin Roosevelt signed off on Executive Order 9066 in 1942, more than 110,000 people were rounded up. Twenty years later, the song evoked pride in this group of hardworking and loyal citizens.

For me, the song was mysterious and foreign, with a lilt of promise in Sakamoto's voice. It's a catchy melody—sung in Japanese—that encourages the people of Japan to keep their heads up and believe in the future. Promoted by a local disc jockey named Sam Schwan, "Sukiyaki" played on our local radio station KYNO every hour in the summer of 1963. This was a favorite of my late father-in-law, Sadao Oda, veteran of the 442nd Infantry Regiment, a Nisei cotton and grape farmer, loyal fan of the hapless San Francisco Giants, carrier of a small transistor radio in his shirt pocket.

I didn't know Sadao Oda back then. I was living across town, a city boy. That summer, I spent most of my time in a neighbor's tree, eating butt-faced plums. But no matter where I was when "Sukiyaki" played—on the radio of a passing car, say—I grew very, very still and listened, as if someone were calling me: *I'm over here, Gary. Over here.*

That would have been my future wife, Carolyn Sadako Oda who, in the summer of 1963, was picking Thompson grapes. She was a farmworker, who without the help of others earned her coins for school clothes.

Hornby's *Songbook* could serve as boilerplate for your own musical reprise. Look in your attic, rummage your closets and, if you're lucky to find them, hug the record albums, cassettes, and CDs of your teen years. I encourage you to travel back in time to when you were first in love, then out of love, or back in love. Scribble your own list of favorites, sing them, mumble them, tap the beat on the arm rest of your La-Z-Boy recliner. At our age, we've got to keep the music going. Dead, we'll have nothing to sing about.

20,000 YEARS OF FASHION, EXPANDED EDITION

By Francois Boucher

ONE CHILLY NIGHT I ASKED MY WIFE OF FIVE DECADES, "Do you think I should join a think tank?" I sipped my St. Pauli Girl, ran a tongue over the froth on my upper lip. I had in mind the Brookings Institution, the Council on Foreign Relations, the Carnegie Endowment for International Peace, maybe the MacArthur people, possibly the Guggenheim people, organizations where male thinkers wear suits and leather shoes, their throats fashionably adorned with either English or Italian ties. The women thinkers? They would resemble Margaret Thatcher or Hilary Clinton in pantsuits. The fountain pens for both sexes? Oh, let's see . . . gold-tipped Mont Blancs.

Carolyn was seated in an armchair reupholstered by a Hungarian master craftsman, a centerpiece in our mid-century living room. In her lap was the hefty tome titled *20,000 Years of Fashion.* She turned a page, not bothering to respond to the noise that had come out of my mouth. I brought my bottle of brew up like a chalice, flirted with the buxom lass on the label, glugged noisily, and peered down at my attire. I was dressed in pajamas. Sleep was not far off.

When I repeated my question, she still didn't bother to raise her head. Finally, at my third call from across the living room, she sighed in frustration and directed her eyes at me—*What?* I had interrupted her revelry of fashions and textiles, the linen worn by the Twelve Tribes of Israel, jewelry cast by Babylonians, heavy cloaks from Armenia, Irish lace, Dutch clogs, Mexican beadwork, Scottish kilts, headdresses from Nigeria, the stone-ground dyes of northern Africa, the early Roman sandal, stone-age Switzerland's weavings, woolen textiles with broad and narrow stripes found in the salt mines of Austria . . .

I had destroyed her concentration and the pleasure of reading. Still, her face brightened, like a flower, and she allowed herself to remember my question about the think-tank thingy. She blinked at me. Her smile became a chuckle that would have known no end, except her phone rang. She jumped from the armchair and left in a hurry. A girlfriend on the phone. She had no further interest in my drunken aspirations.

To improve my status, I moved from the couch to the arm-chair that my wife claims for her own pleasure. I lifted that massive book into my lap. I remembered the last time I'd looked at it. Carolyn and I had read it in bed, ages ago, when we were young and vital, at a time when if I'd brought up a think-tank thingy she would have been full of enthusiasm for my secret ambition to rise beyond my calling as a regional poet with an MFA. Ah, young love.

I opened the book and scanned the pages, beginning with sixteenth-century Italy, when Turkish turbans were all the rage, provided you had a monkey on a leash to accompany you from one glorious room to another. I thumbed through the pages until, as if in a time machine, I arrived at the beginning, when Adam wore a fig leaf to hide his six-incher. Here's what one of the book's zillion paragraphs sounds like:

> If one admits that clothing has to do with covering
> one's body, and costume with the choice of a
> particular garment for a particular use, is it then
> permissible to deduce that clothing depends primarily
> on such physical conditions as climate and health,
> and on textile manufacture, whereas costume reflects
> social factors such as religious beliefs, magic, aesthetics,
> personal status, the wish to be distinguished from or
> to emulate one's fellow, and so on?

My first reaction to this long sentence? I was glad that this history of costumes and fashion had pictures. To read block after block of such prose would make me search for a bottle of No-Doze in the medicine cabinet. Then, after a swig of beer, I scolded myself for my snickering appraisal. Boucher's intellect was on display and deserved patience if not respect. *That old dude,* I told myself, he worked on this book for years! I was secretly jealous of him. He embodied smarts. He had an appreciative soul for beautiful things and could write clearly. I sometimes write paragraphs in which no one can grasp what I'm talking about.

I understood Boucher's duty. He starts from the very beginning—the fig leaf that hid Adam's uncircumcised tool—and ends with the 1980s couture fashions of Thierry Mugler. That's a lot of history, even for the serious-minded who know a thing or two about textiles and haute couture. To me, this is a book that was meant to be viewed, not read, like a picture gallery in which the museumgoer leans toward a painting on the wall, looks and looks, then goes on to the next artwork. Boucher backs up his arguments with illustrations, photographs, maps, and graphs, plus lots of explanations if you follow the text. This I learned: we humans never grow tired of adorning ourselves, making ourselves fresh, flirting with extremes, showing off, separating ourselves class-wise from one group or another, and confusing the public by dressing outside our conventionally assigned gender roles.

Early on we liked what clothes brought to the body: warmth and beauty. Imagine a caveman returning from the big hunt, a saber-tooth tiger over his shoulder. His wife greets him, a string of mastodon molars around her neck. She smiles and says something like "Zakcruoff kiihal mo mo zow," which, roughly translated from a lost language of the Mongolian steppe, means, "Dear, what do you think of my new necklace?"

Lots in this book to stitch into your memory: the Paleolithic period (600,000 to 160,000 B.C.), think nakedness and fur; the

Mesolithic period (8000 to 3000 B.C.), think fur and animal hides; the Neolithic period (3000 to 1000 B.C.), think animal hides and early weaving; Bronze Age (2100 to 1000 B.C.), think early use of wool along with woven and decorated garments; Iron Age (1000 to 50 B.C.), think woven and very complicated garments, including the two-piece swimsuits worn by adolescent girls who dipped their toes in the Tigris River.

And I noticed this right away: men and women dressed to the nines when making offerings to the gods. They didn't dress sloppily, in the jeans and sweatshirts of their time. The statuettes of the late Minoan period represent important figures in darling cinch-waisted outfits. At religious festivals and palace galas, the costumes are again elegant—obviously for the wealthy and those in position. And wait, I just read this! Around 1750 B.C., men *and* women wore loincloths but then, almost overnight, the loincloth for women stretched into a skirt, a very short skirt apparently, the flirty little things.

Clothing fashions first began when Fred Flintstone roamed the earth. And did we learn anything from our ancestors? Doesn't appear so. Stand in front of a mirror, poets and writers, and you too, retired professors with shirt buttons in the wrong holes. *Gads,* you'll think, in that moment of reflection, *Am I wearing a faded university sweatshirt?* Or, *Is this the L.L. Bean plaid shirt I bought in the 1990s, when I was married to my first wife?* Those Birkenstocks should be flung into a landfill! And that baseball cap? Your team hasn't won a ring since Jimmy Carter was in the Oval Office.

A book like *20,000 Years of Fashion* is not a rarity in our house. We have three bookshelves dedicated to similar titles. My wife is a high-level clothes designer, with a limited customer base, namely me. After all, I must be prepared—and well dressed, at the minimum—if our landline rings and the voice on the other end is the executive director of an East Coast think tank.

SELECTED POEMS
By T.S. Eliot

A NOVELIST ONCE QUIPPED AFTER READING "THE
Waste Land," *Beautifully written but I don't believe a word of it.* This
made me chuckle, the tide of G&T sloshing against the sides of
my cut-glass tumbler. I rattled the ice, peered into the drink, then
instructed myself to re-read this poem that I hadn't considered
in thirty years, a poem that begins "April is the cruelest month"
and ends with (no joke, followers) "Datta. Dayadhvam. Damyata.
Shantih Shantih Shantih."

A late Estonian poet friend—the best man at our wedding,
in fact—spoke like that when he had one too many. He would
drink sloppily, usually in his backyard, sometimes in my backyard,
and then crumple to the grass. Face down, he would slur Estonian
poetry that sounded like "Datta, Dayadhvam . . . rosebud,
rosebud."

Eliot's poetry, with its use of ancient languages, reminded me
of a caption in a movie whose title I don't recall. But the caption,
delivered in a deep voice, went like this: "Truth is like poetry . . .
and you know everyone hates poetry." That got the audience howling. After that, we just sat in the dark, unmoved by a so-so movie.

"The Waste Land" is no fun at all. Maybe the novelist has a
point. And why is Eliot's anger directed at April? Because of tax
season? The pollen count? Weeds rising from the cracks in the
driveway? His pant legs dark from waves rolling on shore? I'm sure
a professor in every state of our nation, including Puerto Rico and
Guam, has answers to my questions, but this influencer doesn't
know any of them.

On that April day when I revisited "The Waste Land," I drank
my drink and fixed another. I didn't find the month cruel at all;
in fact, the San Francisco Giants were inching up in the standings.
So, I sipped my refreshed G&T. I reflected, like a mirror. I was
born in the glorious month of April—on the twelfth if my readers

want to know. Plug that date into your gray matter and remember that I aspire to be on friendly terms with Dom Pérignon P2 Rosé. A case of that good stuff would make me happy. My street address is listed on the Internet.

The next day your influencer got to work. I thought and thought, sober-minded, with my cat twitching his whiskers at me. *Does literature influence behavior?* I asked myself. I decided that I would do a little research. For a day—just one day—I decided to become a full-fledged curmudgeon.

Get grumpy! I hollered to my inner self, be like T. S. Eliot! If I shared a long face with the world, I might make an impression on it. Word on the street would then spread—and the word, once monolingual and suddenly polylingual, would reach universities and institutions, maybe even the MacArthur people. Yes, the MacArthur Foundation! I could see it, a big truck backing into my driveway to deliver $300,000 in twenties. I love that image. Gobs of money and a certificate of honor, some declarative gibberish about my genius. I would glance at it for a few seconds and then store it in a shoebox in the garage.

To that end, I dressed in black and drank my morning coffee black. Black leather shoes and black knee-length wool coat. My eyeshadow? Black. I also instructed the remaining black hairs on my scalp to do just that—think black. I even contemplated chewing Black Jack gum. My goth cat, all black except for his white paws, led the way by walking slowly from the room, pulling a hearse-like shadow behind him.

I put joy aside and left the house full of self-pity. (A secret only for the ears and eyes of small-press readers: I'm a writer of regional importance, a dot among larger dots on the cutthroat literary landscape. As such, I am occasionally considered for prizes, which have eluded me decade after decade. One major prize—won't mention it here because maybe it'll still come—was awarded to another Hispanic poet of slim literary talent but hauling on his shoulders an ego hefty as a wet burrito. He lives in Fresno, doesn't live in Fresno. He's sort of a slam poet, then he's not a slam poet. He's overweight, then so fucking overweight he can't fit his *nalgas* in a car. He teaches and attends faculty meetings, and I don't have to.)

Dressed nicely, I felt the urge to admire my recently bought handsewn Italian loafers. But I forced myself to alter my mood. Instead of a sad violin meowing an easy-listening sonata in my heart, I summoned an entire orchestra of lament and sadness!

Passing along the street in this dark cloud, I was followed for a short distance by two waddling Canada geese. Then they found a bag of half-eaten Cheetos far more appealing and stopped for good, while I continued. Often on my walks I come upon quirky subjects worth sharing with my wife (and now with you, readers). A story suitable for an influencer? If so, be advised that this is truth, not fiction.

I was strolling near the Berkeley Rose Garden when I heard a muffler pop. When I turned, I narrowed an eye at a ratty Volkswagen Bug, a convertible, tooling up the street. I wasn't pleased with that cheerful noise. I wanted nothing to supersede my dark mood. I was busy with my self-pity, the color of ash, which had filled me with unhappy thoughts—*Why had that Hispanic poet been chosen over me?* I sniveled. When the car slowed at a stop sign, I noticed a German shepherd in the passenger seat, wearing a red kerchief around his neck, with his head tilted back. The dog was eating an apple! Yes—a dog juggling an apple in his chops, a miraculous moment showcasing superb doggie talent. How he managed without his paws I'll never understand.

My heart leapt, the ash inside me blew away! Then I saw that the driver was munching an apple as well. What a hopeful Sunday, with a blue sky and a few clouds, and these buddies—man and man's best friend—off on a carefree drive. They were using their minutes of life wisely.

I turned my attention back to the German shepherd. Our eyes locked for a moment, two minds meeting on a public street. When the driver started up again, the car chugged and shuddered, sending the apple tumbling from the dog's mouth. It rolled into the gutter, this apple with all the DNA of joy. The dog looked at me again, briefly, with what I can only describe as a smile. (I'll have to ask our daughter, a veterinarian, whether dogs smile.) I hurried over to the apple, toed it with the tip of my shoe, saw teeth marks and dog slobber. It was the best thing I was going to see all day. I watched the VW bug turn the corner, muffler popping.

I spit out my black chewing gum. I became a frisky pooch wagging a tail. I moved the apple up from one of my least favorite fruits to my favorite. I couldn't wait to get home, bare my teeth, and chomp into a crisp Fuji apple. For one goofy moment I wondered whether I could lie on the couch and eat it without the aid of my hands.

Sometimes when I'm in a somber mood, I remember that dog and his apple. I had been awarded a prize called Joy, while Eliot, the great poet, author of "The Waste Land" and the even more depressing "J. Alfred Prufrock," got the Nobel Prize in Literature. *Hijole*, the truck that backed into his driveway must have been enormous.

A LITTLE HISTORY
OF THE WORLD
By E.H. Gombrich

LAST WEEK, WHILE MY WIFE WAS AT A SEWING
retreat, I sought out this book. I'm preparing myself for the end
of daylight savings time, when the sun disappears behind a line
of trees and the stars appear before I set out the soup spoons for
dinner. The cat will claw and meow at the front door. If he gets no
response, he will cry at the back door. The heater, rumbling below,
will send warmed air upward through three ducts until it reaches
me in my comfy armchair.

This influencer hankers for darkness. It allows me time to
read and mix a proper drink an hour earlier. Is it too late to learn
more about ancient history? I'm already acquainted with Neanderthals, those lumbering foresters who kept their distance from
humans. They resembled us except they were hairier, had stronger
jaws for chomping on bones, and were shorter and thicker in
build, more like running backs. They were from the valley of
Neander, now a part of Germany. They mated without romance
and died in blizzards or from tumbling off cliffs in search of
rabbits, long-horned deer, and edible roots anchored in ice-hard
earth. The Neanderthals invented tools: sticks to hold those
rabbits over a fire, stone axes to break the snouts of onrushing
bears, and the wheelbarrow—clever ancestors.

I could study humankind, of course. But now, with the
summery light vanquished, I'm pausing to consider nature as
a subject worth boning up on. I'm unfamiliar with foliage, for
instance. Last summer a child held up a flower and asked, "What
genus is this?" I twirled the stalk and answered, "The yellow bloom
group." I pointed to another cluster and replied, "Those are from
the white-power flower group." I led the child to the lake. With
confidence I remarked that the moon is responsible for making
waves pitch upwards to tremendous heights and for making men

21

go crazy on Friday nights. I told this neighbor child that my beard stands up when I pull laundry from the dryer—static electricity, you know, along with the ghosts of the Industrial Revolution.

The sun wheeled, darkness spread, and the winds of autumn removed strands of my hair. The day was nearly over when the child asked, "What star is that?"

"Which star?" I asked, standing near the apple tree in my yard.

The child pointed. "The one next to Polaris, just outside of Orion's belt."

Was this a genius with a Sanrio Band-Aid on his elbow? I bit my thumbnail for deep rumination and replied, "That there, Sonny, is the Lucky Star."

The wind picked up, taking a few more strands of hair, the ones I considered bangs. I sighed and named this sigh Shame. I do not possess even a GED in time or in planets. Let Cassiopeia shift, roll, spin, or hurl—whatever she can do to fill the black holes of my education.

Gombrich's history fails to touch upon folklore—a pity. Had to wonder what our early efforts at chewing the fat around a Neanderthal campfire were like. What stories were made up to scare children, for instance? I sometimes return to cautionary stories of my own childhood, Chicken Little and the Big Bad Wolf. They're worth pondering, I think. It's too bad the Three Blind Mice and the Tortoise and Hare are absent from the historian's storyline of our human nature. I would have enjoyed his interpretation of Humpty Dumpty's tumble. Was that big egg nothing but an omelet slapped down on a plate next to hashbrowns and two strips of bacon?

With daylight savings time soon over, I may bone up on myths and folklore. Or I may narrow my interest to everyday creatures that tread on all fours, such as my cat, who is presently napping in my recliner. He thinks he's me. I have known him for 16 years, but he has known me, in cat years, for 103. At least this is what I calculate from my position on the carpeted floor. I move from an easy yoga pose into a deep stretch, hand gripping the knob of my big toe. When I meow from slight pain, he opens an eye, assesses my presence, and closes that eye. Opening both eyes to watch me would just be too much trouble.

In our reversed roles, he in the comfy chair and me on the floor, there must be another cautionary tale. Am I nothing but an older man, or do my bushy eyebrows signal the start of a new species? Or could these eyebrows represent a gene left over from Mr. Neanderthal? I'll have to read *A Little History of the World* thoroughly to see if it was possible for those genes to have traveled over the centuries into my own polluted bloodstream. For now, I recognize my genetic history as backdrop. In my standing yoga pose, I'm shadow and light. That's all some of us can be, shadow and light. I'm a doer of no great deeds, powerless to induce a meow from my cat. He won't bother to open both eyes for me.

I pour myself a drink. I raise my glass and toast the end of daylight savings time.

GREAT TALES
FROM ENGLISH HISTORY
By Robert Lacey

I WAS IN SEARCH OF BLOODLETTING TO COUNTER
my anemic morning cereal, which featured one-percent milk and a
mushy banana. I checked my bookshelf, eyes moving left to right,
up and down, until they fell upon *Great Tales from English History*.
I pulled it out, blew dust from its spine. In this book—with headings
like "Elmer the Flying Monk," "King Canute and the Thieves,"
and "A Prince of Thieves"—the history, invariably bloody, rages on
every page. I lowered myself into our comfy armchair, scanned the
table of contents, and began my quest on page 978, when Ethelred
the Unready was wearing the crown.

As the prose was lively, I would have been happy to spend
the entire day rediscovering Olde England, but I soon came
upon the sought-after passage, something to counter the effects
of an old man's bowl of cereal. The story involved Sir William
Collingbourne during the rule of Richard III. The year was 1484.
My interest? The treatment of *poet* Sir William Collingbourne,
who penned a satiric rhyme directed at the king. He then further
enraged the authorities by nailing it to the doors of St. Paul's
Cathedral.

Bravery, I thought. *What bravery from a poet. I could learn from him.*

I closed a fist, I feigned anger. Me, I wanted to be brave as
Collingbourne, to shout at world leaders in faraway time zones,
for instance. But against whom? Trump? Putin? Netanyahu?
All three. Would they give a shit? Would my name make a wanted
list? Would I be put under surveillance? *There!* the CIA would
mutter into their miniature walkie-talkies, the size of breath mints.
There's Gary Soto, aisle 3 at Grocery Outlet! And there he is
again, at O'Reilly Auto Parts. The KGB, in turn, would hunt me
down at a sad little farmer's market offering only squash and limp
string beans. But Netanyahu would send a tank after me—the guy
is over the top.

Poet Collingbourne's taunt was considered treasonous. When he got wind that the king's soldiers intended to jail him, he smartly rode away on a horse and hid in a nearby village. But he was loud there, too, drunkenly bragging in a tavern about his satiric ditty. He was discovered, jailed, spat at, ridiculed, slapped around, and so on. Then he was hauled back to London, where townies lined the streets and reveled in his public disgrace. A judge called for his execution, all because of a slanderous poem. The poor fellow was strung up on the gallows (Execution Dock at Wapping, I believe), brought down while his lungs were still heaving, then castrated and disemboweled.

But Collingbourne was a wit to the end. When the executioner shoved a hand into his abdomen to pull out his slippery entrails, he reportedly groaned, "Oh, Lord Jesus, yet more trouble."

I touched my own belly as I considered the brave poet who spilled his guts for authoring a seditious poem. I'm no doctor and have no idea how the body works except that the mouth opens, the mouth closes and chews, and the throat swallows. So, I imagined that the cereal in my stomach was turning into some sort of energy and returned to Great Tales from English History. I read with enjoyment, with horror, with laughter. I learned that England was once part of continental Europe. But with the global warming then in effect, around 10,000 B.C., the sea rose and separated France and England. And two countries would remain forever separate, culinarily speaking.

I next read about Britain's oldest complete skeleton called "The Cheddar Man," a name which has nothing to do with cheese but refers instead to the location where his remains, skeletal legs tucked up in fetal position, were discovered. This would be in Cheddar Gorge near Bristol. He was a hunter-gatherer who had a penchant for eating wild horses, a delicacy right down to the hooves. He also set traps for vermin and rabbits and clubbed wild animals that were nearly as tall as he—his skeleton tells us that

Cheddar Man was short. He dwelled in a cave and enjoyed a fire that lit the walls and darkened them with soot. He was a family man who died tragically young, the experts say, from a whack on the head. And the marks found on his skeleton were not unlike the cuts a butcher makes when separating meat from bone. Cannibalism? These same experts say that few human skeletons exist from that time, because families often ate their own. They cracked open the bones of Dad or Mom, little brother Ug, and little sister Uga, and sucked out the marrow.

As a momentary anthropologist, I picture dinner around a small fire. The family, minus the breadwinner, is sitting in a cave. There is only small talk because their brains are small, maybe— let me guess—the size of a golf ball. The fire warms Mom and her two children, the nucleus of the modern family. (Let's make this around 9000 B.C., when England first became an island.) *Survive*, Mom told herself, survive by any means.

I see Mom looking up from the fire, her eyes stinging not from her husband's death but from the smoke of roasting meat, and saying to her son, "Ug, please pass the cheddar, Man."

CALIFORNIA DMV
EXAM WORKBOOK
By Eric Miles

YOUR INFLUENCER WAS ONCE FACING A BLEAK DAY
in early February. I had just had a batch of poems rejected by a
literary magazine from the Northwest, a staple job presumably printed at a local copy center. The winter sunshine had
disappeared from my eyes. My mood was dark as Proust. Then a
letter arrived from the California Department of Motor Vehicles.
I sniffed it. It, too, smelled of photocopying. I sat in our comfy
armchair and uncapped a St. Pauli Girl. The letter used my
legal name, Gary Anthony Soto, and had my correct date of birth,
street address, blood type, and instructions for what to do with my
polluted organs in case of a grisly car accident.

I swallowed something that tasted of fear.

At age seventy-three, my time was up.

My wife had been required to take the written driving test
in the previous year. I wasted no anxiety over her performance,
mainly because she's smart and studious and will remain smart
and studious long after I start drooling into a Styrofoam cup.
My confidence shrank. I looked online for practice sites. The first
one offered free tests in fifteen languages. *Free* was a word that
I could get behind. Like a mushroom, my confidence grew overnight. *This is going to be a cinch*, I told myself.

But of twenty-four questions I missed nine, a failing grade.
I pictured myself wearing a dunce hat, sidelined from the traffic
of life. Without my car, where could I go? And how? I didn't want
to be one of those geezers who struggle to board the bus. I loathed
the image of me biking to my gym. Or walking. *No*, I told myself,
I could never walk around in a blazer and slacks, my usual
getup. *Thumb a ride?* I chuckled at the scenario that played inside
my head: an indie film, featuring a poet who accepts a ride from

an inked-up crazy and disappears. Ryan Gosling would play me. My on-and-off girlfriend would be Barbie. My steadier girlfriend would be an age-appropriate Annette Benning look-alike who works as an astrophysicist at Cal Tech. Thinking fast, my darling Annette cuts through all the bureaucratic bullshit in D.C. and alerts the president that the country is in deep doo-doo: space monsters will arrive in pairs by the end of the week. The president then writes on a Post-It, "Monsters, doo-doo."

I bought the *California DMV Exam Workbook* and, like a rabbinical student, studied with great concentration. I was forced to put aside my current reading—*Quite Early One Morning*, by Dylan Thomas—and refresh myself on speed limits, double lines, single lines, colors of lines, when to dim your headlights, curbing wheels, making left turns, pedestrians in crosswalks, the use of hazard lights, freeway speed limits, the rights of bicyclists, school buses with flashing red lights, times when it is permitted to drive on the shoulder (never, it so happens), curbs painted red, blue, green and white, texting, driving under the influence, high beams and fog lights, use of the horn, merging onto freeways, train tracks, signaling, snow on the road, U-turns, and grogginess that requires the driver to pull over and sleep. Eric Miller, the author, saved my ass—all for the price of $16.95 from Amazon. I aced the test, provided my fingerprints, and smiled at the camera.

And I also discovered something else. Because I had looked online for practice exams, I was barraged by ads directed at retirees, ads that offered furnace inspections, discount rug cleaning, two-for-one oil changes, etc. There was even one called "Burying a Loved One on a Budget."

Eric Miller's workbook got my brainwaves going. I wondered whether poets and writers should have their own workbook, instructions for their own rules of the road, like breastfeeding your new boyfriend while in the commuter lane, changing radio stations from wimpy-ass NPR to totally cool country-western, chucking half-eaten burritos from the car window, smoking a joint while parked in a handicap zone, leaning on your horn at asshole drivers, picking your nose (a male thing), taking off your bra because it itches (a male and female thing), and tooling around town with a chihuahua on your lap. But playing games on your phone? No. Flossing your teeth while turning the corner. No. A bobblehead Buddha on the dash. No.

After I passed the test, flying colors, I returned to *Quite Early One Morning*. The book is pitch-perfect, a classic. But I would never, ever have gotten in a car with Dylan Thomas—a great lush and favorite of mine—behind the wheel.

ON NATURAL SELECTION
By Charles Darwin

"NOTHING IS EASIER THAN TO ADMIT IN WORDS THE truth of the universal struggle for life," the evolutionist begins in a tidy summation of his ideas. These notions were revolutionary when published in *The Origin of Species* in 1859 and are refuted by Bible-thumpers to this day. And yet who doesn't side with Darwin? We humans struggle for breath and heartbeat, food and water, warmth and shelter, and will do anything to keep ourselves alive. At this moment, I'm in love with our cherry tree, which was planted by my wife two years ago. Among its limbs hang the sweetest flowers, white with a tinge of pink, flirty in the way mini-skirts are, and, like us, temporary. Bees will visit the flowers and do whatever they do. Heavy with powder stuck to their furry selves, the bees will be off to pollinate another tree and keep the habits of life going.

This is my science for today. I sort of know how pollination works, and it works beautifully. The single worker bee circling the cherry tree is now doing figure eights. It'll get its bearings and make its way to the Santa Rosa plum with its own white flowers, its own teasing nature—Me, the tree says to the bee, *touch me.*

But nowhere in *On Natural Selection* does Darwin mention *sentiment,* as in becoming sentimental over shrubs, grasslands, and trees in nature. I have a lemon tree that worries me. It's skeletal, twiggy in the center, almost leafless, like an old man bent over with a cane. It was robust when we bought our house thirty-five years ago, with seasonal lemons bouncing on the branches in the slightest wind. Now it's early spring, cold still. In anticipation of its final withering, I bought and planted its replacement, a tree that came up to my knee four months ago and is now waist high. Is it normal to feel for trees?

We have a neighbor who visits the redwood tree at the edge of our front yard. She'll hug it like a bear. She will clasp her hands together in prayer, and place an ear against the trunk, as if listening for its heartbeat. At first, I considered this display silly. In fact, I recall snickering as I stood in the kitchen and watched her embrace the tree.

Now I know otherwise. On the day my best friend was murdered, I was hiking among trees in a nearby park. I spread my arms around the tree and teared up. The life of my friend was once like the life of this tree, a breathing guest on the planet. But with two bullets in him, he was no longer with us. His blood spread on the ground but didn't crawl very far.

Have I evolved? From mid-March until a few days ago (April 21 to be truthful), I have kept my eyes open for the last perfectly cupped daffodil, a favorite flower of mine. It was in the front yard, a showoff until the end. I cut that daffodil and let it wilt for a few days, remembering my dead friend. Then I placed it snugly in a book from my shelf, as if to mark a page.

The book is *The Flowers of Shakespeare*, compiled by Doris Hunt.

SELECTED POEMS
By Robert Frost

YOUR INFLUENCER HAS A BEDTIME STORY.

Once upon a time my wife was in the comfy armchair and I was on the couch, a couple of bottles of St. Pauli Girl on the floor. There was very little light outside, very little light inside, but bright sunshine inside my thick skull. The cat, who'll figure in one of the paragraphs below, was in the kitchen staring at the refrigerator.

"Carolyn, you want to hear a really good poem?" I asked. I held up a copy of Robert Frost's *Selected Poems*. The 1960 publication featured the poet's big head on the cover.

She looked up, then looked back down at *America's Traditional Crafts*, a book so massive that you could use it to do arm curls and get ripped biceps in a week. When I asked a second time, she released a groan and marked her place in the book with a pencil.

"OK, let's hear it," she said. "Better be good."

And here's what she told me she heard.

The Toad Not Taken

Blah, blah, blah yellow wood
Blah, blah, blah tamale
And blah blah, blah trout
For you blah, blah Yabba-Dabba Do.

She got up from the armchair and sat next to me. She placed a hand over my mouth, muffling my recitation, just as I was getting into a poetic groove. I imagined that my delivery, with calculated pauses, actorly nuances, a brow deep with the lines of wisdom, was totally brilliant.

"Gary," my wife said in a sweet voice, "You're mumbling."

I removed her hand from my mouth. I blinked at her, confused.

"Mumbling and slurring your words," she advanced with less sweetness. She picked a leaf from my hair and placed it into the pocket of her apron. "Were you in a tree?"

I shook my head and thought, *Clever me!* I'm doing two things at once. I'm multitasking! "You think," I asked, "I'm mumbling *and* slurring? And, no, I came down from the tree years ago, my relatives too."

She chuckled a little. "Are you sure," she asked, "the poem is called 'The Toad Not Taken'?"

I put her in my lap, the one part of our ventriloquist act that I could employ if I ever did poetry readings. I smiled and said, "I never said that."

"Yes, you did."

"No, I said, 'The Toad Not Taken.'"

"See, you said it again." She got out of my lap, her affection for me temporarily over.

I admit that I mumble and, depending upon the hour of the day, slur my words. I'm a poet for my own sake and not for the sake of others. I never do poetry readings, lecture, teach creative writing workshops, or show up to college classes as a surprise guest and preach to the students about getting real jobs, that sort of thing—not counting the time when a judge sentenced me to community service. On that occasion I was forced to bore inked-up juvenile offenders at a facility not far from home. Byron, California, if you want to know. It was no fun watching young gangsters yawn in my face.

"Seriously, Gary," my wife said. "I don't think the word *tamale* is in the poem either. Or 'Yabba-Dabba Do.'"

"I never said those words." I cast a glance at the poem, righteously confused. *Where? Where were those words?*

"Or 'trout'," my wife added. "They were on a road, not at a fishing hole."

Laughing, I absently kicked one of the empties at my feet. I cracked my knuckles, smiling like a pumpkin, and tried to remember how long we had been married—was it forty-eight or forty-nine years? I considered placing a hand over my wife's mouth and asking her, "See? See how it feels?" I considered her move to shut me up as something close to censorship.

I admit that I have listened to my recorded voice and didn't like it one bit. I don't possess an actor's voice, though if I did it would be along the lines of Brando in *The Godfather* when, for instance, he says, "Make him an offer he can't refuse." I would want that kind of voice, something husky.

"Gary," my wife continued, after picking up one of the St. Pauli Girl bottles. "You're slurring because you be drunk." She winced at the buxom fraulein on the label. "Her top is too skimpy."

"Skimpy has come back into style."

"Is she famous? Does she have a name?"

I swigged my beer and searched the ceiling for an answer. I found one and said, "The Venus of Bavaria."

"You be drunk!"

I pouted at the lass on the beer label, then smiled at my wife, comparing and contrasting the two women who figure in my life. I said, "You be talkin' East Oakland funk."

"Yeah, fool, words you be understanding."

Our game, our way of entertaining ourselves late in life. Other times I yodel in Fresno Okie slang and other times Spanglish. Brooklyn Hebrew? I tried it once, but it didn't fly.

Then the cat came into the living room. He parked his butt in front of us and said, "Meoooow."

Carolyn scratched his head and rang the bell on his collar, this wife of mine who minutes ago was entranced by a book on textiles. She was now sitting next to me again. She hesitated, then asked: "Is the cat drunk?"

"What do you mean?"

"He's slurring his 'meow.' Did you put beer in his water bowl? If so, I'm going to get really, really mad."

"No, I didn't give him any beer. You know I don't like to share."

I considered the cat and, as if on cue, he said, "Minou-minou." For a micro-second, I wondered whether he—sartorial cat dressed in a tux—had developed a slight French accent. After all, he was friendly with our neighbor's poodle.

When I went into the kitchen, the cat circled my feet; the little guy knew I was about to open the fridge and brighten his life. And this I did. I fetched him a handful of bologna and got myself a beer. I sized up the fruit bowl: apples and a few oranges, bananas spotted like leopards, an avocado, a lemon with its perpetual seeds, the cornucopia of healthy living, all because of the low prices at Trader Joe's. Back in the living room, my wife read "The Road Not Taken," enunciating this five-stanza classic as clear as the cat's bell.

Got to say, Robert Frost, big head and all, be the man.

THE DISCOVERY OF THE LARGE, RICH, AND BEAUTIFUL EMPIRE OF GUIANA, WITH A RELATION OF THE GREAT AND GOLDEN CITY OF MANOA, WHICH THE SPANIARDS CALL EL DORADO, AND THE PROVINCES OF EMERIA, AROMAIA, AMAPAIA, AND OTHER COUNTRIES, WITH THEIR RIVERS ADJOINING

By Sir Walter Raleigh

GOT TO WONDER IF A SUBORDINATE, SAY A MATE first class, mopping the floor of a massive seagoing ship, might have paused from his work and asked Raleigh, "What are you working on these days, mi-bucko Commander?" Would he have answered, "The Discovery of the Large, Rich, and . . . blah, blah blah." His tea would have grown cold by the time he finished answering the question.

The book was written in 1596 or so, while Raleigh was in the West Indies, and not in the Tower of London where he was later jailed on charges of treason against King James. (His imprisoned years were 1612 to 1616, I believe.) There, in jail, he married Elizabeth Throckmorton, one of Queen Elizabeth's maids of honor. There, he fathered a son that he named Carew. There, he wrote *The History of the World*, a much tidier title. Outside, the Thames River must have resembled spilled ink, dark and thick, on which ships laden with cargo slowly pushed out to sea. On the river, ducks clacked their beaks and poked each other's eyes.

A squealing pig might have slipped out of a farmer's arms and taken its chances in the river—anything to avoid a long knife run up its belly. The pig would have drowned and floated away with its trotters set straight in the air.

In Raleigh's late winters, the sky must have boiled with ink-colored clouds and dyed the miserable townies a color something like ash.

SAMUEL PEPYS
By Claire Tomalin

WHAT DID I TAKE AWAY FROM THIS BIOGRAPHY?
A few literary details that I will quickly forget.

Samuel Pepys, civil servant and memoirist, was a rogue outside the marriage bed. His first wife was Elizabeth, and their servant girl in the year 1667 was Deborah Willet, or "Deb," just out of her teens. Pepys, age thirty-three, was smitten with Deb. He enjoyed her youthful beauty, her ability to play cards, and her flirty presence when they traveled, with Cambridge often a destination. In love, he became bilingual: his engorged member demanded that he speak in Spanish and English—Spanglish. In his diary, he wrote after scolding Deb for poor grammar, "I did give her good advice and beso la [kissed her], ella weeping still; and yo did take her, the first time in my life, sobre mi genu [on his knees] and poner mi mano sub her jupes and toca su thigh." Later, when Deb left the household (Elizabeth had put her foot down), Pepys frowned, heartbroken at the loss of his plaything. He tracked her down days later and perfumed the air with romantic stuff. He wrote in his diary after an excursion in his coach to what we might call Lovers Lane, "tener mi cosa (his dick) in her mano, while mi mano was sobra su pectus (a little Latin thrown in) and so did hazer [sic] with grand delight."

But Elizabeth found out about Pepys's excursions—had she attached spies to his comings and goings? A servant who tattled? Elizabeth screamed as most sensible wives would scream. She forbade his leaving the house unless chaperoned by their mutual friend, Will Hewer. Repentant, Pepys agreed to her terms and, to cement these terms, he made love to his wife, then fell on his knees to pray to God for guidance. When he rose to his feet, he saw that the upholsterers had finished redoing their bedroom. That put him in a good mood—such finery in a troubled time of marriage. He didn't speak bilingually again for a good many years.

THE WORD EXCHANGE:
ANGLO-SAXON POEMS
Edited by Greg Delanty and Michael Matto

I DIDN'T KNOW I WAS A TRANSLATOR. I PICKED UP the book and scanned a few pages. A faint memory returned, the image of a crisp letter from Michael Matto, professor at Adelphi University in Garden City, New York. He had written to ask if I would do a few translations from Anglo-Saxon. This was in 2009, around the time when I first began to mumble. I recall visiting my wife in her sewing room. She looked up with pins clutched in her mouth. She took them from her mouth and barked, "What?"

What was a good way of starting a conversation after what had occurred the previous night in our living room, something regarding a six-pack of St. Pauli Girl knocked over like bowling pins. I was my slurring words as I argued with her about the location of the Easter Islands. Were they north or south of the equator? And who owned those islands? Also, followers—this is, like, really embarrassing. Drunk, I told my seamstress wife that I had come across an Internet theory that claimed space aliens had once occupied the Easter Islands. That was when she went to bed.

But I didn't want to bother myself about the recent past. It was a new day filled with hope. I picked up a pin that had spilled from her mouth. I informed her of my good literary news. She took the pin from my hand and sort of listened. I repeated the news: "I'm going to translate Anglo-Saxon poetry." And then I told her things that might have sounded Anglo-Saxon, whole sentences, to which she said, "You're mumbling."

"Like Bob Dylan?" I asked.

She considered the comparison. "Yeah, like him. Now move, space alien. You're standing in my light."

Suddenly we were back on speaking terms, and I had a project. I drank a third cup of coffee to get the brain going.

Anglo-Saxon poetry, I thought dreamily, envisioning Vikings rowing up the Thames, A.D. 980, and scaring the crap out of the townies. Around the campfire, the Vikings would employ their enemy's arrows as toothpicks. I grimaced at an image of the slaughtered citizens of London Town, fire crawling up wooden churches, plunder loaded roughly in the hulls of long ships, and the Picts, an ancient people, hiding in forests, so afraid to come out that they became extinct. (The Picts were not big people. They weren't brave. They would leave only bronze bracelets, shards of earthenware, and their bones. When they disappeared, no one bothered to look for them.)

An early recruit for the project, I couldn't wait to get started. Rough translations were provided, and, in the end, I worked on riddles, a form of poetry often associated with primitive people. They were enjoyable to render into contemporary American English. I did one riddle after another. Here are two from that final collection.

The Wind Sends Small Creatures

The wind sends small creatures
From the other side of the headlands:
Feathery as grain, fine as smoke,
They arrive dark but brighten to chirm and clamor.
They are many, an army to themselves,
Angling for the green pond but not touching down.
We folks know them from a distance,
Salute them with hands over our furrowed brows.
As they toot the language of trees,
We recognize a common song.

(answer: starlings)

41

At Rest, Laborers Lean on Me

At rest, laborers lean on me,
Then lead me to the barn
To pitch feed at drooling cattle.
I'm both tooth and nose,
A hurtful thing if you're a barking dog.
I herd chicken droppings to the fence,
Scratch the garden's terraced rows,
And drag the fields for an early summer harvest.
On my prongs, I lift wheat into a golden pile.
A hero to the laborer,
I return home riding on his shoulder!
If you look closely, you'll see smeared bee and moth,
Maybe an errant flower,
Just past blooming.

(answer: rake)

I have also translated a Neruda poem for Ilan Stavans' *The Poetry of Pablo Neruda*. Otherwise, I have stayed away from translating, for I possess only talent enough to bungle my own poems and not the works of larger talents.

THE RESIDUAL YEARS
By William Everson

THE SUMMER OF 1973, I STOLE THIS BOOK, STOLE
it twice. I left the library with the book pinched between my
forearm and armpit, then returned to tuck it back into the shelf.
The next day I came back to complete the theft. The book was
mine for good; it became a favorite and the centerpiece of my
slender library. I studied the poems, scanning one after another,
mouthing the lines under my breath. The book peeled back my
birthplace—the San Joaquin Valley—with its quiet commentary on
place and agricultural labor. In truth, it was more than a book
about labor and place. It was the first poetry collection that mat-
tered. It instructed me in the use of verbs, sentence constructions,
line breaks, stanza breaks, imagery, and honesty. At that early age,
twenty-one, I wrote on a manual typewriter, my pounding itself
something like labor. Was Everson a major literary influence? In
some regards, I was not only a book thief but also a literary thief.

Everson began writing poetry in the 1930s. Here's what it
sounded like.

Fog

The gray mask of the fog, the pale plate of the sun
The dark nudeness of the stripped trees
And no motion, no wave of the branch:
The sun stuck in the thick of the sky and no wind moves it.
The sagged fence and the field don't remember
The lark or her mate or the black lift of the rising crows.
The eye sees and absorbs; the mind sees and absorbs;
The heart does not see and knows no quickening.
There has been fog for a month and nothing has moved;
The eyes and brain drink it,
But nothing has moved for a number of days;
And the heart will not quicken.

43

I borrowed from Everson, but had my own weather report, my own youthful eye for detail. Here's *my* poem titled "Fog," written in the summer of 1973.

> If you go to your window,
> You will notice fog drifting toward you.
>
> The sun is no stronger than a flashlight.
> Not all the sweaters
> Hung in closets all summer
> Could soak up this mist. The fog:
> A mouth nibbling everything to its origins,
> Pomegranate trees, stolen bicycles,
> The string of lights at a used car lot,
> A Pontiac with scorched valves.
>
> In Fresno the fog is passing
> The young thief prying at a window screen.
> Graying my hair that falls
> And goes unfound, my fingerprints
> Slowly growing a fur of dust—
> One hundred years from now
> There should be no reason to believe
> I lived.

I'm alive, stiff from sitting in a chair for too long. This morning, I took Everson's *The Residual Years* from my shelf. I opened it up, read a few poems, then studied the book itself. Here's what I found: the card held in the manila pocket at front indicates that the book was checked out in an unidentified year on August 28, September 7, October 2, October 9, March 25, May 11, and many other dates, an indication that the book was passed from hand to hand until it happened upon my thieving grip. Turn the page, and a review says this: "A great deal of modern poetry has been complicated, intellectual, and unmotivated, and people weren't reading it any longer . . . These poems are not abstract, aesthetic objects, but the utterances of a living man." In the preface, Everson writes of this 1948 publication, "The earliest of these poems were written in a labor camp for the unemployed in 1934, aftermath of the world's First Great Depression. The latest was written in a labor camp for conscientious objectors in 1946, aftermath of the world's Second Great War." He goes on to thank Kenneth Rexroth, and the editors of magazines and anthologies where the poems first appeared. None of these publications is any longer around—not one.

I sigh at the poet's bravery. He knew hunger, he knew seasons, he knew craft. Then I remembered something about the man: William Everson, a Christian Scientist in childhood, one day experienced a Catholic conversion. In 1949, he joined the Dominican Order. He shed his birthname and became Brother Antoninus, done (temporarily, at least) with public poems in favor of private prayer.

SAMUEL JOHNSON: A BIOGRAPHY
By Peter Martin

LITERARY HISTORY OF HIGH ORDER. I SIGH IN admiration for both the subject and the author of an immensely pleasurable biography. I don't know how scholars can remember what they remember. So, my report after two glasses of wine, with a third on the way.

For Samuel Johnson, home was often the tavern, at least during the day. His place of honor was a chair by the fire, "the throne of human felicity." The fire lit his large and unhandsome face, with flames dancing in his pupils. An uncommon wit, Johnson held court, bantering with a mix of low and highbrow. When he had to relieve himself—he was partial to wine, though daily drained multiple cups of tea—he aimed at a bowl in the corner, one so pungent with other patrons' urine that he might have winced at the smell. Or, if not the bowl, he might have used the street, his hand screening his member.

Do I have literary history right? That he was once relieving himself when a washerwoman scolded, "Dr. Johnson, shame, shame! Your dick is sticking out!" In mid-stream, he turned and quipped, "Woman, don't flatter yourself. It's only hanging!"

Taverns and coffeehouses were his homes, his universities, and perhaps his places of worship, sanctified by the incense of wood smoldering on grates. Candles sputtered on tables, and windows rattled from carts rolling on the cobbled street. Dogs slept off their hangovers in corners; they, too, were partial to old-fashioned ale.

Johnson arrived in London in mid-March 1737, with Davy Garrick, on a hired horse—one man rode the horse while the other kept up on foot. For a week, they had alternated back and forth—Johnson on the horse, then Garrick on the horse—all the way to London Town, where they quickly parted. Each had his own destiny in front of him.

Johnson is famous for the quip, "If you have tired of London, you have tired of life." I'm not certain if he agreed with this sentiment in his early days, or even his later days. He probably made the comment after receiving a commission from a publisher. London was loud, dangerous, crowded, filthy, but nevertheless the place to be. I recall a scene in Boswell's biography when the great man, with a similar scholar in tow, fretted the cold night away by walking London's streets, their exertion keeping them warm. They had no place to bunk, no table on which to lower their heads for sleep, no fire over which to rub their hands for heat. They walked until the sounds of carts and horses on the cobbled streets began again, an indication that the taverns would soon open, near daybreak. How Johnson must have sped to the hearth when he first entered an establishment, so grateful for the warmth of its friendship.

A portrait of a man in love with books and words in the right order? I would say so.

MISS MANNERS
MINDS YOUR BUSINESS
By Judith Martin and Nicholas Ivor Martin

A SCARY REALIZATION AT AN HOUR WHEN I'M ON
the couch, drink in hand, and watching shadows crawl up
the wall—no, your influencer is not suffering from delirium.
It's just the hour of the day and the hour in my life when I admit,
with sadness, with regret, that I have never worked in an office.
I never had to put on a coat and tie, peer down at my wristwatch,
and hurry off to a job by public transit. I am far removed from
the bosses and employees, cubicles, photocopying, phone calls,
PowerPoints, deadlines, Zoom conferences with a team in Hong
Kong, and decision-making that allow businesses to legally rob
the clueless masses. I imagine office workers seething with hidden anger, muttering under their breath: "Fuck, I hate my boss!
He belongs in the paper shredder!"

I sigh with sadness, regret, and shame that I have managed
to avoid office work. I close my eyes and see it all on the screen
in my brain: water coolers, fax machines, deadly meetings, charts,
flirtations, gossip, ass-kissers, poor spellers, dead plants on the
windowsill, the beeping of a microwave every thirty seconds,
FedEx deliveries, and strangely, on Taco Tuesday, two employees
hanging an assistant manager by his heels out a window. The fall?
Sixteen floors if the lackey doesn't hit the canopy first. Then, it's
only fourteen.

"If you'd bought us the scanners, you wouldn't be in this
position!" one screams.

"Yeah, and we asked nicely, too!" blares the other. "You have
life insurance, don't you?"

These are my images of office work, along with employees
riding silent and uncomplaining elevators. What did I miss?
It's all in a book I found in one of the Little Free Libraries that
stand soldier straight on Berkeley streets. I have admired the

levity of Miss Manners' books on etiquette and this one, slightly dated, brings business culture to light. It offers quandaries that employees face. The authors (mother and son?) answer real questions—at least I think they're real and they are certainly plausible. They are witty, wise, considerate, and full of common-sense. The questions range from when does romance become sexual harassment to who among your colleagues should you invite to your wedding. Company loyalty? It's there. The demeaning CEO? He's there. The colleague let go before lunch? He's also there, and lots and lots of questions answered with authority. *Miss Manners Minds Your Business* is a page-turner, and one that we should follow to the letter.

But we're human. It's difficult to follow advice.

I can't recall a single contemporary poet or writer who has worked in an office. Is there a reason? I swallow a lozenge of truth and don't like the taste one bit. We lack commonsense, enthusiasm for moving papers around, attention to numbers (unless it's a check addressed to us), patience, or aptitude for soft-ware systems. Plus, we sometimes weep for no apparent reason, hug trees, and forget our passwords the minute we create them. Why would we be welcome in an office? Most literary types would consider taking the potted plant from the windowsill and breaking it over their own heads, then file for workmen's comp.

But, as an influencer, I can't be hasty. I've pondered our absence from office life for the better part of my second drink. Why don't we MFA graduates work in tall buildings, manage businesses, gossip like other people gossip, wear suits and pantsuits, scramble (over other bodies) up the corporate ladder, and pocket free pens, paper, and erasers? We're muscular, we can climb, we like pushing buttons. Perhaps it's time to infiltrate the corporate world. And it wouldn't hurt us if we woke early, showered, put on fresh clothes, did our hair in the mirror—morning preps to show we're normal. To that end, I'm preparing my followers for work. Here is a list of questions that came to me just after I moved from scotch to St. Pauli Girl.

1. By accident I stapled my tie to the desk the moment my supervisor came into the room. What should I have done? I did take a pair of scissors to my tie, but I don't think that helped my image. Worse, I'm coming up for review next week.

2. My boss keeps messing up "it's" and "its." Should I tell this clueless mass of fatty tissue to read some books? And this boss has been hitting on me. His breath smells.

3. I ate a colleague's donut that was sitting on a counter in the lunchroom. I know, I know, I shouldn't have—stupid me. But I couldn't stop myself. She asked, "Who ate my friggin' donut?" When I shrugged, crumbs fell from my chin. She knows I did it. Should I buy her a new donut?

4. One of the women in my office uses loads of perfume. She smells better than most, but I sneeze whenever she passes my cubicle. How should I handle this?

5. I'm a vegetarian and everyone in the office is meat-eating God's creatures. I want to tell them it's disgusting. A bad idea here?

6. I was asked to be part of an interview process for a new hire. It was going pretty good for this woman, then one of her false eyelashes fell off, just like that. No one said a thing. She went on and on and then left with a big smile. I went into the conference room later and the false eyelash was still on the floor. I left it there. Was that the right thing to do?

7. This guy named Bradley brings his dog to work. He says it's a "service dog" and the dog wears a vest that reads "service dog." But it's not! It's just a weenie dog. And

get this, the dog's dick is longer than most guys I've been with. The sucker drags on the floor when he walks around snooping on us. It's so, so disgusting. Should I complain to human resources?

8. When I got fired, the office gave me a party. Was that normal?

9. This person with hair that goes all the way to her butt writes poetry. She found out that I write poetry and now she shares her poems with me. They're soooo bad. For instance, she thinks that the word "cosmic" rhymes with "wrench." That's how stone-deaf she is. How do I make her stop giving me her stuff to read?

10. This person named Peggy is forever trying to sell her jewelry to us. She says that she's going to donate the money to a good cause. Big liar! I want her to stop pestering me. Us. Any advice?

11. When is it right to floss your teeth at your workstation?

12. My officemates knew I was running for the elevator and all the people in there were looking at me, some were even smirking. And I know one person, I think her name is Clare, was giving me a bye-bye wave as the elevator door closed. I was hurt! Is it OK if I never talk to them again? The creeps.

Poets and writers in the corporate world? Maybe, maybe not. It could supply us with a direct-deposit paycheck, and you all know that would help to settle our tabs at the local watering hole. Plus, we might find material for poems and stories, maybe even a novel if we can stomach our characters who are CEOs, not MFAs. Keep this between you and I . . . no, I mean between you and me. Am I thinking of a great literary work set in the corporate world? No, I'm just thinking of all the photocopying we could get for free.

A YEAR IN PROVENCE

By Peter Mayle

I'M AN INFLUENCER WHO NEEDS TO STAY PUT, focused, and answer questions that will make life better for my followers. This is my purpose in my later years. Still, I occasionally itch to travel. Japan had been on the horizon. Inland Mexico, Peru, and Turkey—particularly Turkey, because when I was in eighth grade I whispered into a pretty girl's ear, "You exude feelings that remind me of Istanbul." I doubled down on my love for her by splurging on a bag of Fritos. To show me that she liked me, she bought me a can of Mountain Dew.

British author Peter Mayle and his wife Jeanne succumbed to their itch to travel. They became expatriates, a word that suggests berets, Parisian cafes, and political leanings to the left. They bade farewell to Devon, England, shipped their dogs over to France, and started a new life in Provence, which offered summery light even when it wasn't summer. How ambitious of them, both middle-aged, monolingual (though they were studying French), and timid confronting new neighbors, most of them country people, though Parisians often own second homes in the region.

The English couple purchased a 200-year-old farmhouse that was once only one large room but now stood three-floors tall. On their six-acre farm grew vineyards and cherry trees. Vistas provided views of other farms and clouds rolling past. Birds? Lots of them. And stone walls haphazardly built. The landscape resembled rural England, so why had they moved? Let's use the phrase "rat race." Mayle and his wife were eager to escape to a new country.

The title itself alerts us to the book's structure: the narrative begins on January 1, with a meal at a local inn called Le Simiane. On the menu, foie gras, lobster, mousse, beef en croute, cheese and salads, "French" bread, desserts, and flutes of kir before a chilled bottle of Chablis.

The book winds down in December, with frost on the ground, their breath hanging in the cold air. For this hardworking pair, it could have ended with bread, cheese, and wine, for they had failed to make dinner reservations on the last day of the year. However, the chef at Auberge de la Loube in a village called Buoux had a place for them, albeit near the kitchen door that constantly swung open. Still, a happy time for the couple. The chef—presumably the owner of the bistro—was French as you could get. His name was Maurice.

Is A *Year in Provence* a diary, then? No, it is a narrative and a florid one. There is seldom a paragraph without plants, sumptuous meals, a parade of local rustics, newly planted crops, newly harvested crops, or responsible worker bees buzzing from one flower to another. Every three pages a patron is seated before an unpronounceable entrée, with a glass or two of regional wine, also unpronounceable. Mayle reports, "Gourmets are thick on the ground." The French expect a sumptuous meal and boisterous friends at the table; after all, France is a land of gastronomy.

For now, I list, in no reasonable order, things that unfolded naturally in the garden and in the landscape, in the sky, in the kitchen, and in village bistros. Here's a list of words and phrases that may stir your hunger for a different life: sea bass, peppercorns, a stew called *pebronata*, slivers of *magret*, cherry trees, vineyards, pork-based terrine in *marc*, paté of rabbit, boars, thrushes, nimbus of smoke, forest, dogs, the valor of dogs, onions, rain, shotgun, hinges that don't work, tables, boxes, thyme, lavender, cedars, pines, scrub oaks, wild mushrooms, pink champagne, donkey, geese, *crottins* of goat cheese, hipflask, courtyard, aioli, escargot, water wells, roses, chateaux, almond tree, smoking jacket, pomade, the Lebéron Mountains, swirls and eddies. All this—and we're only on page 9!

Mayle and his wife were soon exhausted by physical labor. Plus, the bureaucracy of getting permits to repair the farmhouse. Mayle had plans to write a novel before he began doodling out scenarios of farm life. He felt he was onto something, and he was! The manuscript for *A Year in Provence* came naturally and quickly, beneath, I imagine, a trellis of red bougainvillea. His words became sentences, then paragraphs, then chapters. And then, *voila*, an international bestseller, in twenty-plus languages. The French may have been perplexed. Why the hubbub for an English couple renovating a farmhouse? But readers abroad were smitten. Especially in England, under the impenetrable clouds, with the forecast of rain every three hours. Like, hell yeah, they wanted to get out of town, too.

Provence sounds like a place that I would like to visit, provided I can return home on the same day. In truth, I'm not much of a traveler. I like my house, my own space, this couch, my wife's comfy armchair, the rug where I will occasionally plop down to do a couple of yoga poses and tell myself that I'm healthy because I can touch my toes. I count my fortunes by ambling in my yard and walking around the house dusting spiderwebs from the ceilings. Here's a list of my amenities: comfy armchair, couch, microwave oven, stove, pretzels, a sack of uncooked frijoles, Cheetos, rice, kimono on the wall, DeLoss McGraw originals, Campbell's Chicken Noodle Soup, peanut butter, vacuum cleaner, floor wax, pickup truck, radio, landline telephone, Vicks Vapo-Rub, mismatched gardening gloves, canned corn, geraniums in a pot, watering can, rat traps, bamboo, Japanese maple, towels, hardwood floors, a library, coffee grinder, sewing machines, fabric softener, dust mop, quiet neighbors, and—right on cue—my cat. He comes into the living room, sits, and raises a leg that he licks like a drumstick. I think of Mayle's encounter with a hunter named Antoine, who lets Mayle in on the secret of how to cook a fox. First, you need to bring down the fox with a shotgun and then skin it. The tail you can toss.

Food for thought, though not a yummy thought.

I consider my cat, just briefly, skinned and wrapped in aluminum foil, with his paws sticking out. How long would I broil my pet—a dish called *chatte roti*—and at what temperature? What sauce should I ladle over his cooked head? The side dish? That can of corn in the pantry? French's Mustard? I've got a squeeze bottle of that. My cat looks up and sees me eyeing the drumstick of his left leg. He registers the look in my dilating pupils—something's up—and hurries out of the room.

Mayle's book is beautifully written, stylish and warm. It beckons the reader to travel—spend some coins, you tightwad, see the world and let your tongue explore a new language, etc. And if it's France, then you get a chance to French kiss—I'm all for that.

But followers, to be honest, I don't buy into travel. I'm already an international jetsetter. I take a few steps into my kitchen where I find German beer, Spanish olives, Belgian chocolate, prosciutto, pickled herring from Denmark, kimchi, bundles of soba, Oaxacan *mole* from the night before, the world's culinary offerings at my fingertips. That's my kind of holiday, right here on the couch, without leaving the house.

THE BOOK OF TEA
By *Kakuzo Okakura*

FOR A SINGLE DAY, I PROMISED MYSELF TO REFRAIN from beer, wine, tumblers of G&Ts, scotch, or Campari on the rocks—my usual pleasures that begin around six o'clock. I decided to give that saddlebag organ called the liver a day off. I viewed my so-so life and pouted—yes, influencers, too, suffer feelings of regret. You see, I had plans to become someone grand, to change up my same-ole routine. I put on one of my Japanese robes and played the scholar who knows a thing or two about the trickery of the universe. *Be wise!* I scolded myself.

I answered the call right after I ate my morning bowl of cereal. I became Zen-like, austere in thought, slow and deliberate in my steps, cognizant of the flickering tree shadows and the scent of jasmine from the yard, considerate of my wife's selection of Hawaiian music, etc. I decided to continue assuming this Eastern aesthetic *until* I read this paragraph:

> The Philosophy of Tea is not mere aestheticism in the ordinary acceptance of the term, for it expresses conjointly with ethics and religion our whole point of view about man and nature. It is hygiene, for it enforces cleanliness; it is economics, for it shows comfort in simplicity rather than in the complex; it is moral geometry, in as much as it defines our sense of proportion to the universe. It represents the true spirit of Eastern democracy by making all its votaries aristocrats in taste.

After reading this vagary (the second paragraph in a slender book), I could see that the book was beyond me. Moreover, it brought up a memory from the 1980s, when a Tex-Mex poet on the rougher fringe visited me and drank and drank. He offered up cowboy yarns that included moments of yodeling. Eventually, he passed out but not before stumbling out the front door and throwing up. I was on the floor myself, not feeling all that human—like roadkill, to be honest. Still, I listened to the melody of his vomiting and could distinguish a Texas accent as he delivered the goods on an azalea bush. On his return to the living room, he uttered "Romans, Romans," before he lowered himself onto the carpet and fell asleep, still booted up in his shitkickers. What he meant by "Romans" is a mystery to this day.

The next morning, I yanked up this western figure and led him to the couch. I asked, "How you feelin', cowboy?" He had no tall tales inside him. He couldn't explain how he felt. I gave him coffee and a handful of vitamin Cs. To begin the day, I told him how I had taken a class in Japanese tea ceremony the week before. He looked at me, with eyes that resembled pinkish salmon eggs. He blinked dully. He asked, "What? You're drinking . . . tea? Really?" I explained that the tea ceremony respected the subtle nature of hospitality, to which he responded, "Sounds like a bunch of girls take this class." I told him that, no, there were two other guys in the class, though I left out that they had both been attired in kimonos. He then asked, "You sit in the front row and get to look up the teacher's dress?" I told him that voyeurism was not the point, though I did develop a crush on our *sensei*. The poet drank his coffee, picked his nose. "Are you telling me you're vegan?" he asked. "You ain't one of those, are you?" I chuckled and told him that I liked bologna like everyone else. "I'm just saying that I took a class in tea ceremony," I continued, to which he replied, apologetically, "OK, it's cool to expand on shit. But you still like *menudo*, don't you?"

Then I thought of something that might sober him up. I asked him to come to the front porch with me. He followed. I pointed at the ugly splatter under the azalea bush. "Cowboy, you see that?"

"See what?" he asked.

"The neighbor's cat is eating your vomit."

Leaning over the porch railing, the Tex-Mex poet winced sourly and ignored the issue of his spilled guts. "That ain't a real cat," he said. "Dude, you gotta see the ones we got in Laredo! Huge, like leopards. Even rottweilers stay away from 'em."

I own a copy of the revered *Book of Tea*. I keep it around to remind myself of something I don't want to do—or can't do. How could I float through my daily life thinking like this: "Until one has made himself beautiful, he has no right to approach beauty." This Far East mumbo-jumbo does not work when your buddy eats your grub, drinks your drinks, then refuses your generous Zen nature by booting it all into a bush.

A AGA

By Jake Gordon Young

LIKE A BANK SECURITY GUARD, I DUTIFULLY
patrol my bookshelves during business hours. For me, business
begins in the morning with coffee and ends when the shadows
crawl up the wall and the hallway is pitched into dark, around
five o'clock. The smallest book in my poetry collection is written—
no, dictated and illustrated—by Jake Gordon Young, son of Gary
Young, poet and fine-press printer. It measures three inches by
four inches and has a collector's quality to the production: handset
Garamond type, handmade paper called Umbria, hand-bound in
green cloth, and with a decorative label, tiny as a square of confetti,
on the spine. The label reads, *A Aga*. Published in 1992, there
are seventy-five such first-edition copies in the world. It's short
on stature when placed next to *The Complete Poems of Pablo
Neruda*. Still, if Neruda were alive, he might consider the young
poet's first publication, read it in less than a minute, and pronounce
it a rare beginning.

Indeed, rare and a beginning. Master Jake dictated this
book when he was just out of Pampers. His father told me the
manuscript was created in New York while Jake was suffering the
deliriums of mono. At three years old, the child was already experi-
encing a Rimbaud moment. He lay in bed, sweaty from fever, and
yet, art was on his mind. When his father asked, "Can I get you
anything?" the child responded, "Ink and paper."

The storyline of *A Aga* is classic: a very good fellow is riding
a horse and comes upon bad dudes doing bad-dude things. The
good fellow slaughters them. With permission, I quote a passage:

> I saw another bad guy
> and stabbed him
> in his heart
> his chest
> his whole body

There are other such passages, including one about a deer that is eaten by the narrator and a new sidekick from the forest. In the end, the narrator (OK, Jake) finds a girl and lives happily ever after with her.

I plucked this book from the shelf a couple of days ago— actually, it slipped off the shelf when I was pulling out Neruda's collected poems, Neruda with his big, hardbound body of work. I was excited by my discovery. I ran a finger across the cover to dispense with the dust and read the entire collection leaning against my bookshelf. The narrative was so compact that I read it a second time, this time lingering on the drawings. I pondered the creative psyche of Master Jake and how, at age three, he was already familiar with structure—good guy on a journey, good guy confronting bad guy, good guy embracing an amigo, good guy surviving the elements, and then finally, at the advanced age of twenty (for Jake, twenty would have been hella old), good guy settling down with a beauty. I suspect that his father, poet and printer, had read adventure tales to him in bed—the son with a thumb in his mouth, slowly drifting off to sleep, with slaughter and mayhem playing behind his closed eyelids.

We might think this is a cute first effort, a keepsake, a potential heirloom to show the boy after he sprouts into a young man with tattoos snaking up both arms. It's more than cute, though. It wasn't his first manuscript, nor his second or third. It was the result of months of practice, of drawings executed in charcoal, ink, pastels, pencil, whatever struck the boy's fancy. From what I gather, Gary would take Jake to the studio where the monstrous printing presses were kept. At first, Jake was placed in a crib while his father worked. Then the crib was removed, and a comfy chair brought in. To keep busy, Jake drew and, thus, grooved creatively while the printing presses turned.

Gary Young is editor/publisher of *Greenhouse Review Press*. We first met as classmates in the MFA program at UC Irvine. Gary was a year ahead of me, a little more settled (married, for instance, and with an idea of what to do with his life), and had a gentle, artistic side to his character. I could judge this by his penmanship, which was artful and beautiful to behold. My penmanship was clumsy as a kid walking with Pepsi cans smashed under his sneakers.

Gary published his son's book in a limited edition. He has also printed other books, marvelous works, including those of Mallarmé. His books have been collected by major museums in the United States and abroad, particularly Japan. He and his family reside in a forest (this is truth, not legend) and live close to the bone, meaning that things can be tight financially. Such is the life of a poet; for a poet *and* printer, it might be even rougher. He must have thought, on several occasions, of the deer in the forest, and how he might have hunted, like Jake's good guy, for his meat.

In 1993, Gary visited Chronicle Books of San Francisco, which was publishing my poetry at the time. He visited with an editor and shared samples of his fine-press books, including a seductive masterwork of Mallarmé poetry. The editor, though, was taken by a series of relief prints. Here was a coffee-table book, the editor must have thought, for discerning book collectors. The editor was keen on doing a book of Gary's. However, after the numbers were crunched and swallowed, the publisher opted out of the series of relief prints, tentatively titled "Geography of Home." It was too rich a project.

The editor then asked, "Do you have something smaller?" To answer that question, Gary pulled out *A Aga*, possibly from his coat pocket. Chronicle Books, enchanted by its size and authorship, published the pint-sized book a year later. Jake was in kindergarten by then, filling his shoes with sand by jumping up and down in the sandbox. His advance was five thousand dollars. With that princely sum, he could have bought his classmates ice cream for a year.

The book sold modestly. And Jake grew up to be a poet. Once the slayer of bad guys, he now holds an MFA in creative writing. On his graduate-school application, Jake Gordon Young provided *A Aga* as evidence of early publication.

SPARK JOY
By Marie Kondo

A MEGAHIT HERE, LIKE 5 MILLION COPIES SOLD IN dozens of countries and in languages that use alphabets that I don't recognize. The subject: tidying up, as in getting rid of shit. Does her book speak to me? I occasionally do hear a voice in my head pleading for me to downsize. Is this such a moment?

I scan our living room. *Nice*, I think, our comfy armchair in the corner, flowers in a vase, art on the wall, lake view from my window, large mirror that shows me in a good light, and bookshelves packed with more books. My Shinto shrine is set on a tall *tansu*, with packets of sacred rice from the Konko Church. But what is this? A cobweb linked across the shrine's small gate. I could swat the intricately laced cobweb, but I don't believe dusting is Ms. Kondo's subject. She has a higher calling.

Your influencer is questioning his own stash. Is he a secret hoarder? Does he have stuff to shove into garbage bags? He lifts his shoulders with a shrug. Maybe, maybe not. Moreover, does he have to get rid of stuff inside him? Guilt, for instance, or greed, lust, superstition, a burrito eaten on the run?

Marie Kondo's mission is to get you to tidy up your digs. Let's sum up her position, which may be a Japanese aesthetic or a catchphrase to sell books. She speaks of "sparking joy" when we give the heave-ho to the seldom worn or used. Ms. Kondo repeats the mantra—sparking joy—on almost every page. She writes, **"What sparks joy for you personally? And what doesn't?"**

Her use of boldface, not mine.

I scratch the stubble on my chin. I bite my lower lip and think, though not deeply, just enough to pleat my brow in an actorly way. Mentally, I set aside that word joy. I consider the author's approach: the KonMari Method. Her method is more than the process of rearranging a bedroom closet but also peering into your soul to see who you are. Peering down at the ink stain on the front of my sweater, this I can do, but peering into my soul, cluttered beyond belief, I'm not sure. Still, I understand her stance: do your possessions offer joy? She gives us a demonstration of how it works. She says to take a bunch of your shirts and throw them on the floor. Sit on the floor and pick one up, examine it, and judge whether that shirt in your hand gives you joy. Breathe in, breathe out, think clearly, with a smile, with gratitude, with joy. In the final assessment, you can keep one, maybe two, and the others go—and go with this mantra, "Thank you." Thank the shirt for the service it gave.

I have a T-shirt that I don't need to throw onto the floor to judge its worth. I bought it as a prank and wore it a few times on the tennis court and at a freebie ukulele concert in a nearby park. The front reads: **No, I'm not a model.**

My use of boldface.

Ms. Kondo provides an illustration of how to fold undies, T-shirts and socks. When I open my sock drawer, these personal items jump up as if from a jack-in-the-box. *Pick me*, say the black socks—no, *pick me,* say the green pair. Her illustrations of how to fold your underwear made me scratch my head—what does this have to do with me? She has devoted a page to folding a camisole. Now, this was not my worry, nor how to store bras and panties, plus hygiene products. But my two girlie magazines should probably go.

She advocates keeping the lightest things (briefs, for instance) in the top drawers and heavier things (sweaters, for instance) in the bottom drawers. I already follow this rule, but to see it in print confirms my commonsense tactic for keeping things shipshape.

The author has six rules: Commit yourself to tidying up; imagine your ideal lifestyle; finish discarding first; tidy by category, not by location; follow the right order. Is that six? I believe so. If not, that's OK. Just getting started helps. Don't be sentimental, just start heaving stuff into a plastic bag. Like the toilet-roll pencil holder made in fourth grade. Like the third-place school ribbon in wrestling. Like a cadet medal for your service as a hallway monitor in junior high. Like the photo of the cheerleader who promised to let you look at her bush. Like the photo of you eating a soft taco at the Fresno District Fair.

I wouldn't dare second-guess Ms. Kondo. Her manifesto is sound; we do need to free ourselves of possessions. Otherwise, we might be featured in one of those television programs about hoarders with 3000 empty egg cartons in their living room (a societal problem in the Midwest, I learned from the Internet). I pause, reflect and pause again, biting my lower lip. I see that she isn't a bibliophile. She posts her hands on her hips. She preaches about getting rid of books. I've done this on occasion and without mercy, chucked them metaphorically over my shoulder. And even sometimes without that metaphor thingy—just chucked the suckers, the pages singing in the wind like Robert Burns. Still, I confront her advice, she with millions of followers and I with a dozen or so.

Get rid of books—really? I put it in boldface: **Get rid of books—really?**

I solemnly approach my bookshelf, my own personal columbarium. Once again, I thoughtfully consider my library. I pull out *Madame Bovary, All the Pretty Horses, Modern Mexican Painters*, and *I Know Why the Caged Bird Sings*.

Easy call. *Madame Bovary* stays.

I toss other books onto the rug. *Joy*, I force myself to think, joy, joy, joy, like when a Hispanic poet—the one who can't fit in a car—wins a prize and you're supposed to jump up with joy. Like, fuck that shit, that's not going to happen.

I reflect, I ponder. Is the purpose of books to offer joy? Dostoevsky is a walk in the darkest rain. Proust requires endurance, Henry James a secondary book on grammar, Wodehouse laughter, and Bukowski even more laughter.

But joy?

I dismiss my concern. I hurry up and begin. I take armfuls of books from the shelf. Joy, I ask myself, which books give me joy?

Books by William Saroyan, Sherwood Anderson, Anita
Brookner, Martín Espada, Elizabeth Taylor, Jane Gardam, Carlos
Fuentes, Sharon Olds, Claire Tomalin, Peter Carey, Dagoberto
Gilb, John Banville writing as Benjamin Black, Richard Russo,
Oscar Hijuelos, Miranda July, John A. Williams, Pablo Neruda,
Carlos Bulosan, Charles Simic, Richard Wright, Alice Adams,
Charles Bukowski, histories by the perfectly erudite Peter Ackroyd,
coffee-table books on art deco and Italian frescos, songbooks,
a Hawaiian dictionary, two bibles (one in English, one in Spanish).
I eye a book by Chris Buckley, poet and wit, who has been my
first reader of poems since 1974. He looks at me from the author
photo on the back of *Varieties of Religious Experience*.

Don't, Gary, don't! his face pleads.

My use of boldface.

But you were cruel to my poems! I scold in return.

Yes, because your early poems were runts . . .

And you were never religious, I mutter.

I was too! I have a crucifix in my underwear drawer . . .

I shove the book back onto the shelf, between Pablo Neruda,
a poet he admires above all others, and a poet he doesn't think
much of. Serves Buckley right, I chuckle to myself.

Ms. Kondo is a de-clutterer with a spiritual bent, but she's no
book lover. She has a profession, and so do we poets and writers,
though hers is global and ours are usually in our own zip
code. I agree with her. Let's strip things from our lives. Why the
four screwdrivers, the three sets of towels, the frying pans and
Disneyland coffee mugs, the ugly sweaters, the clunky shoes, the
baseball caps from losing teams, the anti-itch ointment, the
lawn mower, the Che Guevara beret, the two landline phones
in a cardboard box . . .

But books? They stay on the shelf, examples of work made
by poets and writers, brows wrinkled from earthly thoughts,
the seeds of their storytelling a nourishment. Joy? Do they give joy?
No, they give us truth and beauty, words in the right order.

THE CHICAGO
MANUAL OF STYLE

HOLY CRAP, YOUR INFLUENCER'S WIFE IS FRUS-
trated with him. She has pulled out the bible about producing a
book: editing, style, production, and printing. She hands me this
hefty volume. She says, "Some of your book reviews are in present
tense, and some are in past. Make up your mind, Mr. Influencer."

I stall, then beg weakly, "Can you make up my mind for me?"

"No, O.G., you do it—now get dressed."

This I do early one morning. White linen pants with one
of her designer shirts, the one with a tiger print. My socks are
dark blue. I put on my slippers, also dark blue, and lower myself
onto the couch and study the dust motes rotating on their own
universal axis. I wonder to myself what civilization lives within the
dust motes. I wonder whether there's a Pakistan and Mexico inside
the dust motes, maybe extinct animals that a super smart teen
could bring back to life. This occupies my thoughts for a few
minutes before I recognize my purpose for the day. I crack open
The Chicago Manual of Style, which in previous years was simply
called *Manual of Style* before "Chicago" was added. The 1906
edition (the first) was called

Manual of Style
Being a Compilation of the Typographical Rules
In Force at the University of Chicago Press
To Which Are Appended
Specimens of Type in Use

These days, meaning the 1982 edition on our shelf, we
appreciate the much tidier title. We, as husband and wife, recognize this reference book as the last word on preparing a manuscript
for submission and, on rare occasions for poets and writers,
publication. But most days we just give up and quietly put those
manuscripts into a drawer.

I tell myself to get to work. I open the book and remember my wife's morning greeting: "Some of your reviews are in present tense and some are in past. Make up your mind."

But I'm suddenly sleepy, very sleepy. I lie on the couch, my hands interlaced and resting on my belly. When I close my eyes, a burrito floats behind my eyelids, then a basket of freshly laundered socks and underwear, a football quarterback throwing a first-down pass, the extinct animals circling in the dust motes, Sophia Loren in her heyday, the cheerleader who promised to let me look at her bush, my first car, my second and third cars, and finally an image of me as roadkill on the literary landscape. I'm mightily dead, in a fetal position, like one of those Picts English farmers unearth now and then.

Startled awake, I'm a vampire sitting up in his coffin. I rub the corners of my eyes and return to my task. I study the table of contents. Then I turn the page and read a portion of the preface —historical stuff in clear sentences that a fifth grader would understand. I note the manual's structure: Part 1, Bookmaking; Part 2, Style; Part 3, Production and Printing. Clever me, I see how I could add Part 4, but for now keep that to myself. I explore Part 1.

Here's what I found in this section on preparing a manuscript for book publication: Half-title, verso of Half-Title Page, Title Page, Copyright Page, Dedication, Epigraph, Table of Contents, List of Illustrations, List of Tables, Foreword, Preface and Acknowledgments . . . It goes on, this reference book that requires a jolt of dark coffee, and offers clear directions on the use of Appendix, Colophon, Errata, List of Contributors, Glossary, Bibliography, Page numbers, etc.

There's loads more information in Part 2, more than most brains are willing to absorb. I provide some of what's presented here: Floppy Disks (gone, like dinosaurs), Typewriters (gone, like some of the larger icebergs), Spacing, Chapter Titles, Tables, Lists of Abbreviations, Indexes, Stylesheet, Cross-references, Cover

Letters to Publishers (compose in a pleading voice is my advice), Preparing Front Matter, Dashes and Hyphens, Transposition (what's that?), Numbering Pages, etc.

There's lots of stuff to remember. I scratch my temple, crack my knuckles. This time-tested manual is as hard as med school, except that it involves readying yourself for publication and fame (I promise to bring fame up in a bit). There's so much guidance in this book—along with illustrations on the use of @, %, *, +, *, -, =, $, ( ), ?, {}, \, |, ^, /, ?, ~, `, and so on.

Imagine how we come into this world—either screaming like a jay or silent as a toad. Eventually, however, we are expected to understand the above if we want to get our books published. This moves me to Part 3, all eighty pages in this section. It's mainly about design elements and typography, composition, printing and binding, and ultimately our creation, the book, which Amazon can sell back to us. In the end, we can usually judge a book by the cover. I say usually because I've started reading books with lovely covers, become angrily disappointed within a few pages, and ended up moaning, "Good grief."

Are you with me, followers? You see what we poets and writers face? And do you remember an earlier paragraph when I suggested adding Part 4 to *The Chicago Manual of Style*? This would be "Fame," a guide to what to do once you achieve what there is to achieve with a physical book. For me, I see it like this: interviews with major TV hosts; managing your Facebook, Instagram, TikTok, and X accounts; stupidly saying no to Oprah, then writing her people, *Just kidding, LOL*; learning French and German in order to display your continental temperament at the Frankfurt Book Fair; touching-up author photos to remove two of your three chins; attending the National Book Awards and managing the tantrum that follows when you don't win; delivering commencement speeches; choosing a suitable gown for the Academy Awards (mainly for scriptwriters); teaching at an Ivy League school; the humble decorum at the Nobel Prize ceremony; how to say *No* to a hottie while staring at her cleavage; working with a private secretary; forwarding your hotel bill to your publisher; drafting prenups before marrying a movie star (poets, don't worry about this); borrowing yachts from the rich and famous; bowing to a king and queen; tying the Windsor tie; wearing haute couture; signing movie and television options; turning to stamp collecting when you're a has-been; saying no when a younger writer seeks a blurb; rendezvousing with a Brazilian lover who's a foot taller than you; rehabbing in the Virgin Islands; burial at sea; etc.

Not sure if I used "etc." properly. But followers, you know what I mean. And I know what my wife means when she says, "Make up your mind about tense." This I will do later when darkness crawls up the wall at the end of the day and I'm permitted to uncap my first St. Pauli Girl. The Venus of Bavaria and I are going to have a very long conversation.

BERKELEY HIGH SCHOOL
SLANG DICTIONARY
Foreword by Rick Ayers

SLANG CHANGES SEASON BY SEASON, IF NOT
month by month, day by day, hour by hour. Whatever has street
value in the morning can be sourly curdled by the afternoon.
Also, slang terms are the verbal gymnastics of the young and only
the young. The invention of a word (or phrase) by someone over
thirty is unlikely. You have a better chance of becoming Einstein
than an author of new slang.

It's like music, movies, or clothing styles. If you're over thirty,
you're not involved, though men my age, OGs, are making a fashion statement these days. They have introduced the "zipper down"
look. This clueless lot will shuffle into grocery stores with their
zippers down and part of their shirttails sticking out the zipper.
You'll recognize them. The old fools often wear white socks.

In 1974, a poet buddy of mine came up with a word that he
spoke to other MFA students. The word was *scolochos*, which had
a Latin ring in its three syllables. For this poet, the word was ver-
satile. It could mean "too bad," "right on," or "what funny fate."
So, if the poet, driving his scrap-metal clunker, found parking right
in front of a movie house, he would call out, *Scolochos*. Also, if
he couldn't find that parking space, he might utter, *Scolochos*. That
poet and wit, in turn, became a truly great creative writing teacher,
influencing students and colleagues in the grand state of
Kentucky. I recall him telling me that when one of the secretaries
(they were called secretaries back in the 1970s) made a typing
mistake, she (always she) would growl under her breath, *Scolochos*.

It was *scolochos* when the English department was denied
a budget increase by the administration. It was *scolochos* when,
on Monday, the department head found all the typewriters
stolen. *Scolochos* when the football team did this, *scolochos* when the
basketball team did that. I'm also told that the dean of humanities
often used the word.

Now back to this booklet on the use of slang. I read, I turn the page, I read some more. Man, this 2004 compilation is ancient.

Examples, please.

How about "blown up"? Its definition reads, in part, "To get paged excessively." Paged? *Like, what that?* the young fools might ask. Sample sentence: Gary Soto be blown up every hour of every *pinche* day. Feel me, *ese?*"

Or "bootsy," which is defined as "bad, negative, hateful." Sample sentence: "Our *carnal*, Gary Soto, never be bootsy. He a chill *vato*. Floated me five for *mi lonche.*"

Or "crew," which is defined as "a group of friends." Sample sentence: "Gary Soto at the senior center with his crew. Those OGs got all the popcorn they can eat."

Or "gank," which is defined as "to steal." Sample sentence: "Wazzup with Shakespeare? He be in his grave, turning crazy like. Thinks Soto be shiesty, ganking his riffs. Not even."

This book is dated, yet fun. I'm all for fun. I ask the Bavarian *chavala* on the label of my beer bottle, "You like slang?" She winks at me and flutters her eyelashes, the saucy thing. So here are some more dated gems: "annoyo" (to annoy), "baller" (respected person), "breezy" (young girl), "dead presidents" (money, as the faces on dollar bills), "gaffle" (to steal), "hooptie" (old car), "nasty" (tasteless), "patna" (friend), "pinner" (a tightly rolled joint), "rollers" (police), "womp" (to smell bad), etc.

Let's cross the pond of time and put a toe in the waters of the 1940s and 1950s. How about the slang of my grandparents' finest hours on the planet? Smile at "jiminy cricket," "heavens to Betsy," "turtle doving," "flip your lid," "hold your horses," "daddy-o," "heebie-jeebies," all sweet and dandy. Like public attire—the torn-jeans look, for instance—slang has gotten sloppy. In the 1990s, kissing was "swapping tongues." Ugly, so ugly.

And what about the slang of my youth? I date myself like a carton of expired chocolate milk. Yes—we had our own slang in the 1960s and 1970s. It pissed off our parents—and might come back someday (the slang, not the parents). The movies of our time—like, no. The music of our time—those rockers be dead. Our hairstyles— just small polite Afros, *por favor*. Our loose jeans—hang 'em off my butt.

But you never know. I liked clothes in my youth and like them now. (I never wear a sweatshirt in public and never roam Berkeley in Birkenstocks—like, hell no!) Our bell-bottom pants, circa 1973, were outta sight, then shredded, repurposed, and now back in style! What can I say but, *Scolochos*.

THE CHILD IN TIME
By Ian McEwan

ADVENTUROUS ME, I RETURNED HOME FROM THE library with *The Child in Time*, a novel about the abduction of a three-year-old girl and the unraveling of her parents' marriage—guilt, anger, grief, self-pity, loneliness. I'm a quarter of the way through this tidy novel but may return it to the library, unfinished. Words are underlined in pencil by one of the previous borrowers who—let me guess—was trying to improve her vocabulary—"deciduous," "reptilian," "affability," "provenance," "slow loris," "averse," etcetera.

The underlined words have slowed my progress and not because of annoyance. As a poet invariably searching for the right words myself, I began to consider the author of these pencil strikes. I sized her up. She was female, possibly my age (late sixties at the time), and reflective about the years lost on a no-good husband. Like the dainty pencil marks, she was understated in every way—touch, voice, makeup, and clothes. I began to imagine her as a reader of admirably crafted contemporary fiction. Perhaps a nurse attracted to the novel because of its theme—a child abducted and nowhere to be found. Or a psychologist—but no, that was wrong too. A psychologist would have known most of the underlined words, as would a nurse. Maybe an inexperienced bookworm on her way to the morning shift by bus?

I assigned her the details of a life story. A widow, she read the novel late at night, with cotton balls in her ears against the noisy neighbor above, while a moth batted around the lamp and a cat the color of smoke slept at her feet. No—she was an office worker on her lunch hour in a park with graffiti-marked trees and large boulders. A duck with a white ring around its neck was eyeballing her from three feet away. Did she have a crust of bread to quiet its quacking? But no, I was too hasty—she was a florist in rubber boots, her breath condensing before her in the cold, with a surplus of roses in tall buckets to sell by late afternoon. Any later, and their heads would have begun to nod downward.

Conjecture, all of it, but one fact remained: a reader had underlined words. In doing so, she embraced the notion that learning doesn't end. She may have been a mail carrier padding about in corrective shoes (this is how I saw her by page 180), but she was not about to give up on her head, now capped with grayish hair.

There are thousands of words we don't know, long or short, soft or clunky, seen in print or heard in conversation. We can just let them go, like passersby, and be none the worse because of it. But we also can give new words a try on their own. Who is this person who looks like a *dogmatic* priest? What sort of *fluctuating* shopper is she? Where did they get that *dubious* car? These adjectives may not quite fit the nouns, but the attempts are interesting. Why don't we *forge* the refrigerator? Close, but not quite.

In a recent novel, I paused at this sentence: "'She's fly,' said Mathew to his best friend, Ronald." *Fly,*? I mouthed the word, quietly befuddled. Was this a typo? Did the author mean to say "She's flying?" That wasn't probable because the scenes in the novel were grounded—nothing about planes, terminals, boarding passes, and such. Failing to grasp the meaning, I asked a young man eating lunch on a bench, who said that *fly,* meant lovely or pretty or hot. Then the young man put down his sandwich and informed me that the word was like a Blackberry—no longer in use.

Oh.

I intend to finish McEwan's novel—it's very good, after all. But as my eyes peruse his prose, I can't help but think of the previous reader—nurse, psychologist, florist, mail carrier—as concocting a subplot, a sleuth with a pencil poised. With *affability*, she turned the *reptilian* page and, through thick reading glasses, made little *aversive* checkmarks for her *dubious* self-improvement. Her cat and a stuffed *slow loris* watched with *provenance* from the end of a very comfy and *deciduous* bed.

GABRIEL GARCÍA MÁRQUEZ: A LIFE
By Gerald Martin

ON THE DAY GARCÍA MÁRQUEZ DIED IN 2014, MY shoulders dropped from sadness. I felt teary-eyed at the literary world's great loss. Wasn't the master meant to live forever? And shame on me. When I searched my bookshelf not a single novel of his was embedded among other books of slimmer talent. No *One Hundred Years of Solitude*, no *Love in the Time of Cholera*, no *Autumn of the Patriarch* . . . What, had they flown off like butterflies?

On the shelf, though, was his biography. I turned to this book, turned inward and looked back to late summer 1974, when I read *One Hundred Years of Solitude* in an apartment that felt like solitude. I didn't have much in the way of furniture—bed, stove, noisy refrigerator, kitchen drawer that jingled with spoons and forks when opened or closed. I would soon be off to graduate school, off to an intellectual shore as foreign as Europe, namely classes in unfathomable literary theory. I would read Michel Foucault and, feeling inadequate, think, *People get what he means?*

In the meantime, I read the novel in front of a frantically spinning fan in Fresno's intense summer heat. I was twenty-one, slender but not starving, and so transfixed by the story that I didn't fully grasp the grand experience or the remarkable nature of García Márquez's descriptive energy and wildly inventive narratives. Wasn't most literature like this? No.

I recall gazing up from the novel, sizing up the blank walls of my apartment, and then returning to the pages of *One Hundred Years of Solitude*—the landscapes of flowers, the river with miraculous fish, the exotic birds like fruit in the trees. I read slowly, with quiet appreciation. I was swept away by the story, traveling in my mind to the fictional town of Macondo, where the citizens had a penchant for both melancholia and nostalgia.

Readers, dedicated followers, Fresno in my youth was not Macondo. Nevertheless, I went in search of my own fabulous territory. I biked to south Fresno, where I grew up, discovering the vacant lots where homes had been torn down in the name of urban renewal. Weeds grew in feisty bunches; feral cats hissed from behind the weeds; and dogs, thin as shadows, loped about the abandoned cars, their rims and tires gone, the headliners draped on the seats like failed parachute jumps. I rolled my bike over a squad of chinaberries, and the scent of their broken skins evoked my childhood. My own sense of melancholia built up inside me like one large tear. Wasn't this the plum tree that I climbed when I was six? And this stream of shattered glass, didn't it look familiar? I rolled down the alley, the broken glass like a trail, leading to the 7-Up Bottling Company. That was the place where I, a child feral as a neighborhood cat, had once stood gazing at the mouth of the open building, until a kind employee handed me a soda.

Some of this is fabricated, of course, though the essence is true. It is the stuff of a young poet in search of a subject, a sense of place, his own worth. It is his own Byronic posturing, his own Macondo—minus the Greek islands and the lush jungle of Colombia. Fresno is a hot, flat place, its dry river choked with tumbleweeds and dumped tires. One Hundred Years of Solitude woke inside me a dedication to place. It evoked in me the value of the seemingly valueless. Under this pile of rotting boards could be the story of a large rat with a long tail—no, let's make that the shortest rat with the longest tail. García Márquez did that to me; did that to all young poets. He allowed us to enhance the world as we saw fit.

Three years later, I published my first collection of poems, The Elements of San Joaquin. I so much wanted to write like García Márquez, so why not a title that suggested his influence? My second book was titled The Tale of Sunlight. More García Márquez in the shape of several poems, including "How an Uncle Became Gray," dedicated to the master.

One day he fluttered
Like a neon
With butterflies
That followed him,
A herd of vague motion
He came to think
Was a cloud spread thin
And bearing a blank message of rain.

If these initial lines, written when I was twenty-two, do not suggest García Márquez, then I must've been very clever pulling the wool over the editor's eyes. What do you think, followers?

Little did I know, then, that a novel such as *One Hundred Years of Solitude* does not appear annually, or even once a decade— nor did I understand that the genius that produced such a literary work would parallel the best of William Shakespeare—quote me on this, followers.

García Márquez's personal history begins with a haphazard childhood, raised by grandparents and fussy aunts. Then came university life, journalism, starvation in a real sense, boisterous friends that kept him from work, an apprenticeship as a serious writer through his first years of marriage and his own slow temperament—followed by the lightning strike of imagination that became magical realism.

The bolt of creative lightning struck in 1965, while he was driving away from Mexico City (he and the family were off to a coastal vacation). García Márquez heard within himself the phrase, "Many years later, as he faced the firing squad." The tone of the line struck him—tone being equivalent to an identifiable voice and writing style. His literary duty forced him to turn the car around, head back to Mexico City, and begin work—how his family must have groaned at their return home, without seeing the ocean.

García Márquez began with that first sentence. Immediately, however, he faced difficulty akin to writer's block. In an interview, he confessed that getting started was terrifying. He had the first line and the tone (on paper and in his head), but what should come next? Such terror is not unusual among writers, or the poverty that creeps at its side. While he was writing the novel, his family became very poor. The car, an Opel, was sold, and the items inside his apartment were pawned—television, radio, fridge, his wife's jewelry.

The novel got written, and so many others. We are better souls for his output: *No One Writes the Colonel, Leaf Storm, The Autumn of the Patriarch, Chronicles of a Death Foretold, Love in the Time of Cholera, The Story of the Shipwrecked Sailor*—the titles themselves are poetry! At one point he aroused the suspicion of our government, which denied him a visa because of his friendliness to Fidel Castro. That situation changed, however, when President Clinton pronounced *One Hundred Years of Solitude* his favorite novel. Good move, Mr. President.

García Márquez was a man of letters, a humanitarian, the most righteous among all Colombians, a leftist in world politics. He was a husband and father. His nickname was Gabo (mine is Goyo—pretty close). His territory was Latin America (mine is Fresno). He was the winner of literary prizes. He described a source of inspiration: "I have never renounced the nostalgia of my hometown: Aracataca, to which I returned one day and discovered that between reality and nostalgia was the raw material for my work."

Martin documents the master's life and creative ordeal. I'm just retelling, poorly perhaps, and certainly with embarrassment. On the day García Márquez died I didn't have a single book of his on my shelf. Where had they gone? Had I lent them to friends? House guests? I sigh. García Márquez, your departure was sad. That a mighty cloud of butterflies led your spirit to another place is certain. But your books stay. My regret is that I never touched the hand that wrote them. If I could become a musical instrument, let it be an accordion whose lungs breathe sighs of melancholia.

BEASTS OF THE FIELD
By Richard Steven Street

AS A POET, I'M EXPECTED TO EMBELLISH THE
factual world. By this I mean elevate, depress, rearrange facts, color,
drain the color—all in an attempt to provoke the reader. I've been
at this for forty-plus years. This is my calling—poetry. But on
occasion, I visit the heady world of scholars. I am curious how
this breed handles their subjects, and, particularly, how they stay
focused on a subject without quitting.

For the past three weeks, I've put aside my current literary
project, poems about rivers that go nowhere. I have taken *Beasts of
the Field* by Richard Steven Street from my shelf and reintroduced
myself to California rural labor. The history of agriculture has
never been a pleasant frolic through pastures, orchards, and vineyards; the narratives here are unsettling, if not criminal. The text's
800-plus pages will make readers reach for a roll of Tums. The sub-
title is *A Narrative History of California Farmworkers, 1769–1913.*
If Mr. Street had carried on his research to include the remainder
of the twentieth century, he would have had to report even more
dispiriting hardships of farmworker labor. The behavior of land-
owners in quest for profits has been just plain bad; likewise, the
behavior of Catholic clerics in quest of converts and free labor.
And for many years, business and religion converged into a single,
deadly force.

I will discuss what Street has written; if I get some of the
dates or details wrong, just work with me. Again, I'm a poet and
unemployed, not accountable to a university or other institution
that would place me at the roundtable of high-level yakking.
I intend to tease you into wanting to discover *Beasts of the Field*
for yourself. I begin with Padre Junípero Serra, a former professor
of philosophy, who sailed from Spain to Mexico—a journey that
took several months over the choppy Atlantic Ocean. The year is
1749. He is fifty-five years old, a stubborn religious zealot from the

Franciscan order. He and his fellow priests are replacements for the Jesuits, who have been called back to Spain because they harbored attitudes not in line with those of King Carlos III. In time, Junípero Serra will establish missions in Alta California; three centuries later, he will wear the halo of a saint. But I get ahead of myself.

First, Padre Junípero Serra treks from coastal Veracruz to Mexico City, where he intends further study (he has come to the religious order late in life). He walks in his burly tunic, or rides by mule and horse when they are offered. The vegetation that he passes is green and luminous, teeming with unnamed lizards and snakes, brightly plumed birds, insects in hardy armor, and short-statured Indians who wisely go into hiding. Those Indians who don't run away stare at him as he passes with a contingent of soldiers, rustics, and others in the Catholic order. Serra considers the Indians in their short tunics with beads around their necks to be soulless creatures. The children are nearly naked. The women, a jabbering type. Within Serra's lifetime, he will convert them—if not those he encounters on his journey from Veracruz to Mexico City, then others like them. This will be his life's work—conversion of the native populace to Christianity.

Some higher power, some god other than Christ, doesn't want Junípero Serra in the New World. On his journey to Mexico City, a snake bites his leg, which becomes swollen and weepy with infection. From then on, he walks with a limp. However, he sneers at physical pain, he sneers at death. He arrives in Mexico City, he studies there, and, within a few years, he is assigned to venture forth with lance-bearing conquistadors at his side.

Soon he travels northward. In what would become the state of Texas, Apache Indians try to kill him—their arrows fall short or whiz over his head. In Los Angeles, an earthquake trembles under his feet, the sun bears down on him, and the mosquitoes and other insects nick his flesh until it pops with boils. The padre is invincible. He believes that the renewal of faith—or injection of faith—

comes from self-punishment. He makes no secret of his penchant for pain. He wears a hair shirt, deprives himself of water and food, and sometimes whips himself until he bleeds. His snake-bitten leg never heals; it becomes ulcerous and stinks to high heaven. But his pain is as nothing when he remembers the pain of Jesus on the cross. He is reported to have once lit the hairs on his chest on fire and to have flagellated himself even while giving a sermon. The Indians at his religious services must have looked at one another and thought (in their own languages), *Crazy man.*

In Alta California, Padre Junípero Serra establishes missions, nine in all, with plots of land whose crops will sustain the occupants. The Indians know nothing about European agriculture but are forced to learn. Here is a shovel, the religious overlords tell them, and here is a hoe—get used to them. And this thing, they threaten, is the whip—to add to your sweaty education. This is the attitude of the Franciscan order and the Spanish soldiers. This is not an exaggeration. They brutalize the Indian population. They kill them in vast numbers.

For the Franciscans, pain is redemption, a way to find Christ. The Indians are forced to shed their traditional clothes, to wear pants, shirts and, when attainable, the civilizing footwear of boots. They eat from tin plates. They follow work routines. In a single generation, they lose most of their previous adherence to tribal lore. One Indian from the San José mission will cry, "Padre, take back thy Christianity." They wish the return of their own spiritual totems and stargazing cosmology. A religion in which the head priest flogs himself publicly and makes you kneel for a tiny piece of bread—what kind of savagery is that?

The first farmworkers in California are Indians. They are naturally dark but will become darker than the earth itself. The sensible ones often run away.

*****

The Diegueño Indians killed Padre Luis Jayme, and others, on the *ranchería* of Cosoy, near present-day Old Town of San Diego. The year was 1769. Rumors were like seeds with wings—they had a way of flying great distances. The Diegueños had heard of the missions in Baja California and meant to keep their distance from the Spaniards and the forlorn Indians they brought with them. When a crude adobe church went up, the Diegueños attacked it. The Spaniards hastily built a fort around the church.

This was the first of many attacks. Nevertheless, the missionaries, feeble from sickness, possibly frightened to the point of mutiny, remained. *To hell with your agricultural fields*, the Diegueños must have thought. From time immemorial they had lived on acorns, wild fruits, and berries, along with fish, abalone, mussels, and clams from the bay. Fifty years of skirmishes ensued—a ball from a Spanish musket, an arrow from an Indian. Graves were dug, bodies lowered into the dark holes. Buzzards floated above.

It's still possible to find arrowheads around San Diego's Old Town. Below ground are the remains of Indians of Baja California. Caught in the crossfire, some of these first farmworkers died during the attacks on the Diegueños. They also succumbed to disease, malnutrition, exhaustion, and—it is likely—suicide. Their Christian names were Pedro and Juan, their Indian names unknown. Their native languages of Kiliwa, Cochimi, and Paipai are nearly extinct. Of present-day Paipai, there are 193 speakers; of Cochimi, 80; of Kiliwa, 46. As for the Diegueño, who fought the conquest and did their best to stop the padres and soldiers, there are about 110 speakers, 15 of whom are under the age of five.

As for Spanish speakers, think millions. Hundreds of millions.

*****

I lope ahead, like a burro, to recount the work of the Japanese Mexican Labor Association—or JMLA. Imagine Oxnard at the end of 1903, the horse and buggy era, a time when nighttime meant exactly that—darkness without the light and noise pollution of modern cities. Think of the mighty oaks that dotted the rolling hills around Oxnard and think of men—and some women—as farmworkers. Think of crickets in damp grass and June bugs stuck on window screens, the slap of doors on outhouses, a rooster poised on a shed, and the whinnying of horses in their stalls. Sunrise meant work, calloused palms, and chopping beets in fields that ran for acres.

But before continuing my account of the JMLA, I must, lamentably, accuse the Franciscan order of maintaining their vineyards and fields in the fashion of slavery. Were the Indians often shackled? Yes, they were. Did they receive pay? No; housing and food were their rewards. Did many succumb from exhaustion? The earth knows the answer all too well. Were they schooled? In a sense—they learned from stockades and the ringing of the work bell. After excursions to the San Francisco de Asís, Santa Clara, and Carmel missions in 1794, British sea captain George Vancouver reported that the Indians did their tasks with a "mechanical, lifeless, careless indifference." I could present other witnesses to this mockery of religious life, people like Otto von Kotzebue, Jedediah Smith, and Jean Francois de La Pérouse. They were sickened by the treatment of the Indians, treatment that would carry on into the next century.

Here's Chester Rowell in 1903, writing in an editorial for the *Fresno Republican*: "The main thing about the labor supply is to muleize it . . . The supreme qualities of the laborer are that he shall work cheap and hard, eat little and drink nothing, belong to no union, have no ambitions and present no human problems . . . Some sort of human mule, with the hibernating qualities of a bear and the fastidious gastronomic tastes of the goat, would be ideal, provided he is cheap enough."

Chester Rowell was a civic leader in my hometown of Fresno. He has a school named after him.

89

But this poet has veered off his tractor path. Now I mean to address the Japanese Mexican Labor Association, and the workers who followed the Indians into the fields. These replacements included unlucky miners from the 1840s, Chinese, bindle stiffs (vagabonds of mostly English and Irish stock), Japanese and, finally, the first Mexicans to arrive in California not under the yoke of the Franciscans. Again, we must remember that Street's narrative begins in 1769 and ends in 1913. His stories do not include Filipinos, Dustbowl Okies, Armenians, Sikhs, the waves of Mexicans displaced by the revolution of 1910 or the *braceros*, immigrant groups that, in their own time, would taste the sweaty salt of fieldwork.

Now a little introduction to sugar beets. Many believe sugar can only be derived from sugarcane and is a product of Hawaii and Jamaica—how advertising steers us wrong. Sugar also comes from sugar beets, a crop grown throughout the San Joaquin Valley and the coastal area around Santa Maria and Oxnard. In 1897, Congress passed the Dingley Tariff Act. This act imposed a heavy duty on imported sugar (Hawaii was not yet part of the United States). In it, the sugar magnate Henry Oxnard saw an opportunity. He scouted the land north of Los Angeles and obtained 48,000 acres in Ventura County. This fertile tract was near the Santa Clara River. Mr. Oxnard considered the port city of Hueneme ideal for shipment of his goods.

In 1898, the second-largest sugar beet factory in the country was constructed, with 175-foot smokestacks that could be seen for miles. Boardinghouses were built for the laborers. Settling ponds for polluted water were carved into the ground. Storage facilities for the beets were built, a private railroad laid, water tanks raised, and so on. In a very short time, a new agricultural industry was in full swing. Indeed, the operation was so successful that the Southern Pacific Railroad built a branch line to this acreage and called the station "Oxnard;" thus, the city of Oxnard.

The work, both in the factory and in the fields, was grim. Street details a litany of injuries and deaths that suggest conditions as dangerous as mining. There were decapitations from loose pulleys, hands and arms crushed in machinery, faces scalded from burst pipes, falls from elevator shafts, haulers injured by wagons, fingers sliced by hoes, and drownings in the settling ponds. Noise from the relentless machines was another hazard. The short-handle hoe? You never walked straight again after three seasons thinning beets with what farmworkers called *el diablo*, the devil's tool. As for alcoholism, who wouldn't drink to mellow those evenings?

Chinese immigrants, along with some Anglo-Americans, were the first farmworkers. Thousands were needed as the production of sugar beets was—and remains—labor intensive. This crop requires extensive thinning and weeding.

However, there were insufficient hands for the acreage under cultivation and the rumors of seasonal employment flew up and down California. Soon Japanese farmworkers arrived from Riverside, Watsonville, San José, nearby Santa Paula, and possibly right off boats from Japan. Along with the Mexicans, the Japanese would become the most noticeable—and hardworking—of laborers. The Japanese had a labor contracting system operated by the *keiyaku-nin*, a benevolent society of sorts, one that constructed ocial halls and helped its members find jobs and shelter.

The arrival of the Japanese became worrisome not only for the locals but also for the management of Oxnard's newly named American Beet Sugar Company. The management, in anticipation of union activity, formed the Western Agricultural Contracting Company (WACC). Their aim was to diminish the power of the *keiyaku-nin*, who were seen by non-Japanese as familial, clannish, and secretive. (That they operated in Japanese was itself enough to suggest secretiveness.) The intent of the WACC was to contract workers, Japanese among them, and thus weaken the *keiyaku-nin*. In no time about 90 percent of the farmworkers around Oxnard had been contracted. The WACC gained control, siding in nearly all cases with owners such as the American Sugar Beet Company and its small cousin, the American Crystal Sugar Company. Wages were reduced and work conditions spiraled downward. Who tallied the injuries and the deaths? The graves won't say.

In 1903, aware of the WACC's heartlessness, Japanese and Mexican farmworkers formed the JMLA. In the few photos included in *Beasts of the Field*, none of the workers are smiling. None seem robust or are in the company of women. These are the luckless and the desperate, often shoeless, with their dirty shirts as limp as flags.

The younger Japanese who joined the JMLA had grown weary of the *keiyaku-nin*, who were perceived as paternalistic and indifferent to farmworkers of other ethnicities, namely Mexican and Chinese. Nor was this younger generation friends with the stronger unions, like the AFL. Those groups were—no surprise—full of racism of the most vicious kind. California labor leader Walter MacArthur, for example, said, "I have learned that a Jap can live on the smell of an oily rag."

The leaders of JMLA were J. M. Lizarras, a local farm contractor, and Y. Yamaguchi, an upstart socialist from San Francisco by way of Japan. Officially, the association—not a union, per se—started in the second week of February 1903. Hundreds joined on day one and hundreds more would continue to join, draining laborers from the WACC and the more traditional *keiyaku-nin*.

The breaking point occurred when the WACC insisted that all Japanese farmworkers, including 120 college students from San Francisco, accept lower pay and sign contracts with the WACC. Hundreds of these workers left the beet fields in protest. Yamaguchi wrote a call for action in the *Oxnard Courier*:

"Many of us have families, were born in the country, and are lawfully seeking to protect the only property that we have—our labor . . . It is necessary for the welfare of the valley that we get a decent living wage, that the machines in the great sugar factory be properly oiled—if the machine stops, the wealth of the valley stops, and likewise if the laborers are not given a decent wage, they too must stop work and the whole people of this country suffer with them."

The sugar beet officials must have slapped the newspaper and turned the page, confident that nothing would happen. A mistake, as it turned out.

On Sunday, February 23, Yamaguchi was jailed for parading in the street with the strikers of his newly founded association. He was arrested by Sheriff Edmund McMartin, who believed a riot was imminent—forget the clause in the U.S. Constitution about the right of free assembly. Yamaguchi was acquitted a few days later. Judge W. E. Shepherd probably shook his head at the trumped-up charges.

I picture Yamaguchi blinking from the sun as he exited the small jail that harbored bar brawlers, opium smokers, unfortunate drifters, and petty thieves. I see him dusting off his coat and fitting his hat onto his head. There is no physical description of Yamaguchi in *Beasts of the Field*, but I imagine him as small and round-faced. If he smiles, it's because something good has occurred for the association. The association would survive and grow. How could it not?

In turn, there is J. M. Lizarras, who is described as short and stocky. Aside from these attributes, I paint him with a large mustache—a *bigote*—and with a slow gait that takes him from house to house, bar to bar, and field to field in his recruiting efforts. He touches the sleeve of a countryman from Mexico. He speaks slowly and convincingly. His eyes are soft, his mouth even softer. He shows the farmworker his belt. He points to a notch in his belt and says, "When I eat, I use this hole." The notch is the nearest one to the end of his belt, indicating his satisfied stomach. "When I don't eat, I use this hole." He shows the worker how he must tighten the belt. Lizarras offers better pay, honest representation (unlike other contractors, his association would not abscond with workers' pay at the end of the season), friendship, and respect—because who else toils as hard?

The sugar beet officials sang an old tune. They called members of the JMLA anarchists and revolutionaries. While it is true that JMLA members disrupted a WACC campsite (they cut the poles of a tent or two) and hollered for scabs to leave the field, their protests were not about niceties. Their adversaries, in this case the sugar beet cabal, had the power of the press, police, government officials, and often, though not always, the townspeople. A ragged bunch of strikers with a noble cause, the JMLA struggled to be heard and seen. The association was about attracting others to a cause larger than just their weekly wage.

Here I pay homage to K. Obata and K. Yoshinari, both members of the JMLA. On or around March 10, the two were arrested for shouting at scab beet thinners to drop their hoes and leave the field. Shouting, it appeared, was against the law. I imagine Obata and Yoshinari as two brothers, one just taller than the other but both from the same mother of conviction. They were dragged away and jailed. A week later they were in court. To the dismay of the American Beet Sugar Company, however, the two were acquitted. What was the world coming to when the law couldn't remove rabble-rousers from a place of business? Who was this judge who let them go?

But I also pay homage to the starving scabs, who were brought in as replacements. After judging for themselves the work and pay offered by company contractors, many of them joined the JMLA. I pay homage to Perfecto Olgas, who was shot in the throat by an unidentified Japanese assailant from the WACC. This occurred on March 23, when JMLA members tried to stop a wagon train of laborers. Also shot on that day were Luis Vásquez and Manuel Ramírez, along with two unidentified Japanese. The melee was covered by the *Oxnard Gazette*, which reported that, "The street was crowded with a motley throng of Orientals, Mexicans and Americans. Oriental faces peered anxiously from doorways and windows, every vantage point was filled with spectators and the excitement grew apace." Fifty gunshots were fired in all.

Blood and earth, a not uncommon mixture in labor history. The ultimate victory? An eight-hour day, better pay, and some small measure of respect. The JMLA proved to be headstrong from the get-go. There was no union card, no contract to sign, no pins with worker emblems, no rallying fight songs, no flags to wave in the sugar-scented air. Street describes the relationship between the Japanese and Mexicans as harmonious, based on their common interests. The JMLA set a good precedent for future organizing in the fields.

Yamaguchi spoke no Spanish and only limited English. Nevertheless, he and Lizarras were able to rally more than 1200 members to strike. Soon the cause found sympathy from the townspeople and as far away as San Francisco. I imagine Yamaguchi on a wagon, the horse still hitched up. He has taken off his hat, scanned the faces of the assembled workers—of Chinese, Japanese, and Mexican descent—and swallowed once or twice before addressing the group. He speaks passionately in Japanese, and all the workers move closer. Though most can't comprehend his words, they understand what he is saying. They smell themselves—sweat, beets, earth, and courage—and not one can take his eyes off Yamaguchi. Even the horse turns to look over his shoulder at this man, who has formed an association so that others might live better.

*****

Beasts of the Field was published in 2004 by Stanford University Press. My words here will not increase its sales or academic prestige or even garner much interest in the history of California farm labor. Still, I'm urged by conscience to continue a little longer and ask another question. How could the Vatican canonize Padre Junípero Serra? I couldn't find any miracles in my reading of Serra's personal history, except for the miracle that any Indians survived him. Without the much-anticipated controversy, Pope Francis made him a saint in September 2015. The motive, some insiders believe, was to move away from the Eurocentric saints and anoint a cleric from the Americas. A halo was placed over Serra's head despite the protest of fifty Native American tribes. The Vatican proclaimed, "He [Serra] was a strong protector of the native people." What a laugh!

I side with the Native American tribes. Remember the Indian from the San José mission who cried, "Padre, take back thy Christianity." He followed up this plea with, "I want none of it; I will return to my country."

Beasts of the Field is scholarship of the highest order. As both a poet and a reader, I have some inkling of the work that was required to write this beast of a book. What honors should we bestow upon Richard Steven Street? A professorship? No, let's not force him to teach. Endow him with a comfy armchair so he can stay home and write up a report on California rural labor in the decades that followed. His hands would get dirty at this laboring scholarship.

THE AGE OF AMERICAN UNREASON

By Susan Jacoby

FOLLOWERS, I QUICKLY CONCLUDED AFTER revisiting this book—it was dusty, it was ignored—that the author paid attention in school. By school, I mean college. She didn't nod off in rhetoric or yawn in philosophy. Linguistic typology? She was front and center, with a massive brain like a pulsating sponge. Whenever in doubt on the use of language, she turned to *Oxford English Dictionary*.

Jacoby is an unabashed rationalist. She's a secularist, meaning that she wouldn't mind if we did what the constitution said that we should do—separate state from religion, government from personal lives, that sort of thing. She notes that we're dumbing down our institutions of higher learning. You don't have to be a rocket scientist to side with this truth. However, in 340 pages, she explains what's going on and, moreover, why and what we can do about it.

How smart is Jacoby? Fill your eyes with this sentence:

> If, as I will argue, America is now ill with a powerful mutant strain of intertwined ignorance, anti-rationalism, and anti-intellectualism as opposed to the recognizable cyclical strains of the past—the virulence of outbreak is inseparable from the unmindfulness that is, paradoxically, both aggressive and passive.

That's a sentence that would take two or three breaths to finish, evidence of the book's intellectual vigor. Also, I believe that readers could quickly become accustomed to them. In fact, you may long for such sentence constructions. They make you proud that you understand them. Jacoby writes a clear prose with a clear intent: to remind us of our worldwide intellectual heritage and shake us readers awake. For Aristotle's sake, let's root for learning! Let's defend thought and the result of thought: ideas.

We are basically lazy—Jacoby says we are, and I agree. Education does take an effort and a good many of us, the old and the young, the rich and the poor, are not willing to devote our time to intellectual growth. Here, we mean basic logic and willingness to aspire to grand thinking. And history? History might be the sandwich . . .

I stop here, followers. My wife has sailed into the room.

"Here," she says. She hands me what resembles a crumpled ransom note. But it's a grocery list of the usual: mini-cucumbers, apples, soba, tofu, mandarin oranges . . . And on the bottom of the note, in red ink, the ink of correction, she has in caps WHITE BIAS TAPE. JOANN'S.

I blink. I get my brain pulsating into action. Regarding the last item, I ask, "What's 'white bias tape'? Sounds racist to me."

My wife narrows an eye at me. She says not to worry my silly head about racial issues. Just go to Joann's, she tells me. When the phone in her hand begins to ring, she hurries away.

My task of pulling stuff off the shelf—I can handle this—and the bias tape, no problem. But what's involved within *The Age of American Unreason*. Now that's a challenge that requires hours with your snout in the book. I sit back down in my comfy armchair. I thumb a few pages of the index. Holy, Darwin! There are references to Henry Adams, Mortimer Adler, Tom Paine, middlebrow culture, 'boy brain, girl brain' dichotomy, biblical literalism, human vs. divine authorships, Aristotle, conservative intellectual establisment (*really, one exists?*), Shakespeare, Roosevelt's fireside chats, papal infallibility, John F. Kennedy, Richard Nixon, the anti-vaccine movement, junk thought, repressed memory, fundamentalists, Martin Luther King, Jr., George W. Bush, student protests in the sixties . . .

Do I supply an index to my book, the one in your hands? I wouldn't want to bother you this way. If I did, several more bottles of St. Pauli Girl beer would be required.

But Jacoby, the scholar, provides a twenty-two-page index. You can tell that she knows her subject—thorough, so thorough. The book argues how ignorance is a dangerous thing—look where we are, followers, in 2025, not a hundred days gone and the unimaginable monolingual garbage that spills daily from DC.

I put the book aside, stand up, stretch, and gaze at the lake below—two ducks are sword fighting with their beaks. I sigh at the conflict, the crips and bloods of the natural world? I assert my one truth for the day: Susan Jacoby, a consultant for the Center of Inquiry, a rationalist think tank, is just plain smart. I wish I could offer her a proper drink and have her explain from my comfy armchair the secular nature of white bias tape.

QUESTION 7
By Richard Flanagan

FOLLOWERS, PUT DOWN YOUR TUNA SANDWICH, spit out your corn nuts if you're on a walk. A book that grew on me as I turned one page after another. I'm glad I made this impulse purchase. I've been considering its brilliance since the morning sunlight lit the dining room wall. Now on the wall, afternoon shadows. My senses have perked up. I hear a meow. The cat peers at me from the French doors. Read my lips, I tell the furry guy, you're not coming in! And take a paw and wipe those feathers from your chops!

From my comfy armchair, I file my brief review. Let me praise Flanagan, descendent of Irish convicts shipped to Australia a century ago. The wordsmith can fashion exquisite sentences and whether you grasp his narrative is secondary to the enjoyment of fine prose. Yes, I'm sometimes at a loss, followers. The author is unpredictable, a puzzlement, a maestro with words—true, so true. The narrative is all over the map. He calls up the relationship between H.G. Wells and Rebecca West, the author's visit to Japan where his father was a POW, the atomic bomb, mass suicide on Okinawa during World War II, his family (those alive and those dead), colonial Tasmania, present day Tasmania, the author's education at Oxford—in a voice full of lament.

But lament about what, exactly? My answer is poetic. Flanagan's lament pertains to the infinity of stars, earth, and trees, and his childhood memory of the Franklin River, the very essence of why he writes. How temporary we are, how we're like sunlight on the wall and then shadows in death.

The book, I realize, is not unlike a book of strongly written poetry with specific—and original—imagery. Flanagan is clearly brilliant, has a story to tell, and a readership that laps the shores of faraway countries. I mull over what he might be doing and the hour of the day in Australia, the island of Tasmania where he lives. Maybe he's just like us. Maybe with a bag of corn nuts, he's walking his own residential street. Is this his routine? He takes a walk, comes up with glorious passages, and bounces home to put them down on paper. That would be a nice job.

The book is marvelously elusive, beautifully written, with a stamp of approval from Peter Carey who writes, "*Question 7* may just be the most significant work of Australian art in the last hundred years." Blurbs honk this, blurbs honk that. But here Carey's appraisal is valid. I provide two sentences that vouch for Flanagan's skill if you're not convinced: "After some time there appears out of the mist a car, a Ford Zephyr, overloaded with children and suitcases and bags, driving along a new road in 1963, a muddy dark track slashing a seemingly negligible gash through a temperate rainforest. In this world where the measure of all things is not man-made, it seems at first the merest scratch, a slight wound that will quickly heal over, rather than what it is, the beginning of something gangrenous and fatal."

Again, my report is brief. Here we have truth and beauty, a masterwork worthy of a place on every poet and writer's bookshelf.

THE LYRICS
By *Paul McCartney*

IS IT TOO LATE TO SING? I BELIEVE SO. I'M NO screeching jay on a fence post, no ostrich dipping his snout in a river, no oxpecker riding the back of a rhino. I'm a goose-necked poet who grew up in the sixties, which was defined—for me, at least—by the Beatles. I was a Fresno lad far from the London scene; however, in the 1960s, I was transfixed by the British Invasion and the groovy music that vibrated from my transistor radio. I sported a military crewcut in fall 1963, but by spring 1964 a mop of black hair flopped with each bright step. Paisley was my favorite pattern, "outta sight" was my slang. I was energized by the Fab Four.

Now this gift from my wife, a boxed set that features McCartney's prodigious song lyrics. It's a huge two-volume edition, edited by poet Paul Muldoon, who writes in the introduction of receiving a call in 2016. The voice was some wiseacre pretending to be Donald Trump. That pretense lasted no longer than a few seconds before the voice introduced himself as Paul McCartney. *Yeah, right,* Muldoon thought, probably wondering which buddy was pulling his chain. But it was McCartney. The masterful songwriter asked if the poet would help write up a sort of biography. Muldoon, a poet of extreme talent, was instantly starstruck and at a loss for words by the invitation. Muldoon must have sung a Beatles' tune after he hung up. I mean, a phone call from Paul McCartney—and in the middle of the week?

The result is this volume of historical commentary, inside scoops about the London scene, photos of group members of the Beatles and Wings, images of posters and concerts, old family photos, archival pages of lyrics written on whatever was at hand, and McCartney's personal history, beginning as an audio recording and then put into prose.

Muldoon explains McCartney's literary upbringing: Shakespeare, Dickens, Lewis Carroll, Lord Byron, Edward Lear, nursery rhymes, Robert Louis Stevenson, Gilbert and Sullivan, and, especially, his parents. His father is described as "very good at words." His mother made sure that McCartney kept his snout in books and not in newspaper comics. He was, according to his proud mother, the only kid in the neighborhood who could spell "phlegm."

In essence, McCartney was grounded in literature. There was no social media, no disruptions, just reading material, friends and family. Plus, a quiet neighborhood life.

Then adolescent hormones began to gallop through his veins. He was a teen when the rockers from the USA made parents seethe. There was Elvis, of course, but above all Chuck Berry and Little Richard, the Everly Brothers and Buddy Holly. McCartney's imagination soared. Previously he had tapped his foot to Hoagy Carmichael, Cole Porter, Mario Lanza, possibly the teen heartthrobs like Pat Boone and Paul Anka. Now, in the late 1950s, he had rock and roll and a friendship with a like-minded partner—John Lennon, who at an early age was also penning his own lyrics.

Poet Muldoon knows a thing or two about lyrics (he has authored his own book of rock lyrics). He explains this Beatle's musical approach, describing what he calls the "physics" and "chemistries" of his songs. I go along with the use of these two sciences to expound on McCartney's songwriting. I grasp Muldoon's explanation: physics, I believe, would be how a song is constructed. Chemistry would be the mystery of the lyrics themselves. But there's more to McCartney's creative hocus-pocus— let's push those scientific words aside. Muldoon states that McCartney's songs are structurally like cinematic narratives, as in "Eleanor Rigby," the spinster who will eventually die from a mysterious loneliness. This is just one example of numerous story-like songs. The albums themselves become full-length features. Think of *Sgt. Pepper's Lonely Hearts Club Band* or *Magical Mystery Tour*. Is more evidence needed? *Help*, the album, becomes a movie, as does *A Hard Day's Night*. Let's add the whimsical and kid-friendly *Yellow Submarine* and, near the end of the band's run, *Let It Be*. The Beatles' demise is hard to watch.

Theater takes stage in McCartney's songs. "Mask," Muldoon repeats several times. *Masks* as in theatrical masks. I get this. I believe that literature involves personas, the creation of characters. McCartney's lyrics involve a songwriter masking his own face. He gets to become someone else, male or female, old or young, in love or out of love, happy or depressed. If you're a poet, this is what you do. You provide a mask even if the reader might see the poems as autobiographical. Nothing new here. Poets have always tinkered with truth, songwriters as well. Listeners can ask, *Did McCartney really experience that? Did he really know Lady Madonna?*

McCartney began his apprenticeship in his youth. Apollo, the god of music, inventor of the lyre, didn't wave a magic wand over the boy's head to create musical genius. Instead, at his dad's urging, McCartney started playing trumpet, then soon made clumsy attempts at guitar chords. His first set of lyrics? "I Lost My Little Girl," written in 1956, when Paul was fourteen and grieving the loss of his mother, age forty-seven. Even early on he honored a time-tested strategy—music with a story to tell. This has always been the collaborative strength between Lennon and McCartney, both of whom were influenced by literature, not pop culture. They constructed songs with meaning. McCartney admits that they wrote songs to attract an audience—girls, mainly—but as they matured, they broadened their creative scope beyond "From Me to You," "Thank You, Girl," and "Love Me Do"—all light jingles to be sung while they shook their Beatle mops.

In the early concerts, audiences didn't listen to the lyrics (or possibly even the music). They just screamed—because The Beatles were a "happening." The music was fresh. The adorable boys with their long hair exuded charm and beauty in an England still recovering from war. I have seen vintage footage of their concerts. The crowds were crazy, thick as ants on honey. So thick and crazy that the Fab Four sometimes had to arrive at venues in an armored car. And while I can't back this up, I would say that about three-quarters of the audience were female—and young, very young. I recall an interview in which a security guard was asked, "Was the concert a success?" "Yes," he answered. "Every seat was wet." Wet from the young women peeing their pants from excitement.

Between 2016 and 2020, McCartney and Muldoon met face to face for a total of fifty hours of interviews, with Zoom hours added during the pandemic. This was a massive project—*saludos* to Paul Muldoon. Each of the two volumes is 400 pages and something of a coffee-table book. However, if you delve thoughtfully into the commentaries and hear McCartney's telling of his apprenticeship and his life with the Beatles and beyond the Beatles, then McCartney's literary brilliance is evident, his honesty on cue. The sheer effort alone of assembling photos and then pinning those photos to the corresponding songs must have been a challenge.

I'm nostalgic. I miss the Fab Four, I miss my hair, I miss the homemade guitar that my stepfather sawed from plywood in the garage and laced up with fishing line. That mop of hair, circa 1964, blew out a car window somewhere near Bakersfield, California. Now, I get through the days in a hairstyle close to a military crewcut. At seventy-three, I've got to sigh. Einstein is not around to explain how time has a way of bending out of our lives.

She loves you, Yeah! Yeah! Yeah!

This is what my wife penned on the card attached to the brightly wrapped Christmas present. My other gift was a work of fiction.

RICK STEVES'
GREAT BRITAIN 2004

THE GUIDEBOOK IS OBSOLETE. WHO REMEMBERS 2004? I toss the book into a box: it goes, as Marie Kondo says it must, if it doesn't spark joy. Still, this influencer, slightly tipsy, produces a sigh that wakes the cat. The cat blinks at me, yawns, and goes back to sleep.

I remember the trip to Great Britian in 2004, my wife pulling a small roller bag and I with a slightly larger one. Here's what I remember.

My wife and I were in London for a week before we left by train for Bath, a pretty and touristy town known for its curative waters. According to tradition, you sip from a ladle of spring water at the tap, and you're healed. I drank from the ladle and made a face. Immediately I thought how a pint of ale could make it hella better.

We stayed at a B&B on the famous Royal Crescent, slept in a frilly bed, ate our daily English breakfast, which included tomatoes and kippers, and strolled in mist, for it was early April–cold and short on sunshine.

In Bath we visited the usual sites: the spa, the church, and the wonderful costume museum. We saw a play of Alan Bennett's about an MP who is having an affair–imagine such unexpected behavior from an elected official. I recall one historical home at the end of the Royal Crescent. It was dedicated to life around Jane Austen's time (Austen having lived in Bath). And for the middle classes, if this house was any indication, life had been comfortable. There were ornate plates and cups patterned in Chinese designs, fine cutlery, paintings of the gentry, dainty cordials, the Bible, etc.

In the kitchen fireplace was a wooden wheeled contraption that turned the spit. When a roast was impaled on the spit, a small dog–a Jack Russell, I suspect–was placed in the wheel and made to jog, thus turning the spit. If the dog slowed–or dared to stop–

the kitchen help would spank its rump. The dog's reward for this endlessly circular trot was scraps from the roast and a warm place to sleep.

After three days in Bath, we took a bus to Salisbury, an even lovelier town, with its celestial cathedral, and then to Wells, also with a cathedral that could make a believer out of anyone. In Wells, we enjoyed English tea in a little shop that sold playful teapots resembling pigs or chickens or small cathedrals—touristy stuff, things you pick up and put back down. However, my wife, a seamstress, bought one shaped like an antique sewing machine—silly but cute. After tea, my wife went off to an actual antique shop, also cute, and I had nothing to do but sit on a bench, hands in my pockets from the cold, and watch the activity of a vegetable market, which was nearing its day's end. Because very little was happening, I got up and bought four apples, my contribution to bolstering the town's economy.

My wife exited the shop and pointed to the adjacent store—at least a half hour there, I figured, so, hands in my coat pockets, I ambled along the cobblestone streets. (Later I would understand that I was wrong about the stones. The streets were paved with *setts*—Belgian blocks that are rectangular, not roundish.) I meandered like a lost sheep and stopped to read a poster that announced a choral concert that evening, then a plaque that explained that Wells was named after three wells dedicated to Saint Andrew. This had been around A.D. 704, when Saxons were in control, and King Ine of Wessex was the law. I did my best to input that info into the machinery of my frontal lobe, then returned to find my wife exiting the store with a small package. *Thimbles*, she told me, she had bought thimbles.

Thimbles I could remember.

*****

Wells is a pretty town, a historical town, a friendly town—the townspeople smile and stop to chat with one another, just as they do on the BBC television programing we've seen over the years. We discovered Vicars' Close, reportedly the oldest residential street in Europe, harking back to the mid-fourteenth century. And by "residential" we mean houses lined up with other houses, thus creating a neighborhood, a block, or their word, a *close*. We walked with our purchases (teapot, thimbles, and apples) up this street, which is neither long nor wide, and paved, I saw, with setts.

A girl with blond locks stepped onto her porch to look at us, the first tourists of early spring. Perhaps she had mistaken our steps for those of her mother or a friend or possibly a boy. Her eyes followed us briefly before she went back inside, probably disappointed that it was just *us*, a couple seeing what there was to see. We didn't fret over our tag: tourists. We walked up the street twice because we knew we would never return.

On the bus ride back to Bath, we ate apples, two small ones each, and were delighted by a chevron of geese flying north, flying back home. We watched them until they were faint commas in the sky, then gone. What was happiness but a day in a new place? Then to my surprise, and possibly to my wife's surprise, it began to snow, erasing our footsteps set briefly in two lovely towns.

ALICE'S ADVENTURES IN WONDERLAND

By Lewis Carroll
Illustrated by DeLoss McGraw

WHILE I ADMIRE LEWIS CARROLL'S CAUTIONARY fable, I'm here to file a report because I also admire the artwork of DeLoss McGraw, a sometime resident of Oklahoma and North Carolina. In this handsomely designed book, I turned a page and then another page. I found illustrations whimsical, with a cheerful light. And I needed light to fend off the darkness that had suddenly enveloped our living room. With daylight savings in effect, millions of us had lost an hour—and perhaps even our happiness.

The sunshine was siphoned away and the clocks reset. The cat became confused because the mouse in the furnace closet didn't show up on time. What would Einstein say about these losses? I'll speak for him, the genius with a noodle packed beyond belief and I, an influencer with a ball of Top Ramen that I call my brain. Our conversation was *muy* private, just him and me over the chessboard. This happened on an ordinary Friday. Dr. Einstein communicated with me, provided an answer regarding the millions of lost hours. He believes that daylights savings means we can start happy hour earlier.

What cheer McGraw brings me, what silliness of subjects thrown in the air, what colors and topsy-turvy rabbits—the artist delights in upside-down characters. I pay homage to my friend. He is an artist of enduring charm. Why doesn't a foundation award him a prize? Mr. Google, open your large wallet and dare him to peer into that bottomless wealth. Bill Gates, you do the same. Tell him, "McGraw, you have twenty seconds! Pick out any hundred-thousand-dollar bills you find there. Now go!"

I possess eight of his paintings. One hangs in the hallway. I pass it every few minutes as I move around the house. It's a large pastel of my wife Carolyn and me in the best light and maybe our best years: we're young, standing face-to-face, with our arms coming up to touch one another. There is a fire above Carolyn's head, the genius of love. Here is a marriage done in bright blues, yellows, and reds. The foreground holds a house: love has found a house and will live there for many years.

THE FOURTEEN SISTERS
OF EMILIO MONTEZ O'BRIEN
By Oscar Hijuelos

THE TITLE ALONE ENCOURAGES THE READER TO smile, what, fourteen girls in a Cuban-Irish family? Now this is new, this blending of ethnicities. Readers may weigh this hefty book in their hands—it's a true saga—unaware that what greets them are sisters with sweet romantic tendencies. The oldest weep from their bedroom window at the moon, for instance, while down below flowers toss in the breeze. The author begins the novel with charm and florid detail, with a biplane spiraling from the sky and a handsome aviator emerging from the wreckage. The story is set around 1920, and is divided, like slices of ornate frosted cake, into five servings, all with marvelous details of a domestic comedy.

Oscar Hijuelos is very much an historian of the heart. As with *The Mambo Kings Play Songs of Love*, *The Fourteen Sisters of Emilio Montez O'Brien* is lavishly told. And he seems to dare himself. He writes about a period that preceded his own coming-of-age experiences in New York City during the 1950s and 1960s. Here, Hijuelos travels even further back, first to the 1920s, then decades earlier into the 1880s, with narrative jaunts to Ireland (the O'Brien part) and to Spanish Cuba (the Montez part). Indeed, we get a history lesson, along with the calamities and joys that surround these sisters, particularly the eldest, Margarita, an enchanting flirt. Their father doesn't know what to make of the one-after-another appearance of daughters. True, he and his wife parent them, but he, a portrait photographer and owner of a theater in a small Pennsylvania town called Cobbleton, is boggled. Still, he is joyful and admittedly influenced by his daughters' femininity. The mother, in turn, is more solemn and practical. She has daughters, lots of them, each with slight family variations in personality, each with the talent to sing and create music.

There's no sly (or overt) matchmaking, for she doesn't have time to play the cagey mother eyeing prospective husbands. This sort of meddling hardly comes up, for the sisters themselves know how to attract. Above all, their mother is busy with the domestic requirements of feeding, clothing, and housing her brood. The last sisters are Margarita, born in 1922, and Gloria, born in 1923. This decades-long pattern is broken in 1925 with the final birth: a boy! It's a surprising debut, but over the years, he is coddled and given massive amounts of love. To no one's surprise, this late gift boy-child, Emilio, becomes playfully self-centered and so dashing that he believes that he has a great calling. He likes what he sees in the mirror, that is, himself in all posturing angles. With all the familial adoration, what might he attempt? He becomes an actor, of course, first in New York City and, later, Hollywood, playing such parts as a lieutenant to Napoleon (with few lines) and minor roles in *Tarzan* movies, plus other characters that don't get his name on the marquee.

When I discovered this book, ages ago, I searched my memory for a family as large as the Montez O'Brien family. I remembered the Alvarez family, a large Mexican American family in Fresno, my hometown. The Alvarezes lived in what we called "the projects" and included ten children, with two sets of twins. The first five had "American" names such as Carolyn, Jeff, Susan, Sharon, and (I gulp here) Gary. Perhaps, after reflection, the immigrant parents scolded themselves—these American-named children were dunces at school. The second half of the brood was christened with honorable Mexican names that included Raul, Paola, Aurelia, Beatriz, and Manuel. One can only imagine the identity crisis. Was one half of the family eating white bread, the other half homemade flour tortillas?

I smile, tap a finger against the cover of *The Fourteen Sisters of Emilio Montez O'Brien*—clever, so clever, Señor Hijuelos. Smile, readers, and recall literary history. In the early 1970s, the big three domestic storytellers were the three "Johns"—John Cheever, John Barth, and John Updike—each masterful prose stylists, each with novels that featured families with money, entitlement, Ivy League ambition, decorum; all followers of social registries, all lost after the luster of their social positions wore off. On their own, the characters in the novels of the three Johns turned out spectacularly average.

By the time he was in his early twenties, Oscar Hijuelos was aware of these writers, along with others of the same ilk, and would have gone on believing that these figures were the hallmarks of literature. But a happenstance encounter with a "bone-thin Chilean graduate student" enlightened him. He writes in his memoir, *Thoughts without Cigarettes*, about this encounter—not at length, just a short passage that reveals much. The two were passing time smoking cigarettes between classes, a jive-ass pair talking mumbo-jumbo, with Hijuelos reluctant to speak Spanish, the Chilean stubborn to switch over to English. However, after learning of Hijuelos's penchant for writing fiction, the Chilean began to preach a sermon on the works of Pablo Neruda, Julio Cortázar, and Jorge Luis Borges. Inwardly, Hijuelos was not so sure— *Who are these people?* He thinks he knows one name, but certainly not his work. When the cigarette break ended, the Chilean hustled away, never to be seen again.

The moment was a turning point. I imagine Hijuelos, with smoke unraveling from his nostrils, sprinting up the cement steps of the City College library. There, among the stacks, he locates these writers and others, including José Donoso, Juan Rulfo, Carlos Fuentes, Mario Vargas Llosa, Jorge Luis Borges, and the most stylistically inspiring and helpful, Gabriel García Márquez. These Latin American writers, already world figures, began to speak to him. They became models for his own work and may have even influenced his manner of dress and social demeanor. García Márquez is certainly present in *The Fourteen Sisters of Emilio Montez O'Brien*. In this, Hijuelos's third novel, the descriptive passages edge toward poetry, with preposterous characters and outcomes that force the reader to laugh. The title alone is evocative of Latin America. It's grand and seductive, with a bit of comedy. Who doesn't want to prance side by side with this gaggle of sisters?

While *The Fourteen Sister of Emilio Montez O'Brien* has its literary influences, the work is solely the author's. It is an American novel and, perhaps, a Great American Novel. It tells an essentially American story of familial identity—in this case, the melding of racial groups, Irish and Cuban, along with a father's entrepreneurship and the sisters' penchant for music, romance, and fun.

I imagine that Hijuelos's own childhood was not lost on him. It was imperfect, insulting (he was heckled because of weight and eyeglasses, for instance), and marked by an illness that nearly cost him his life. Hijuelos experienced self-doubt, wars on the street, wars between parents, some drugs and drink, some hip posturing when he was a teen, musical interests (he played guitar), disdain for his neighborhood, love for his neighborhood—in short, confusion. What writer is not born from confusion?

Occasionally, Hijuelos was prodded to Sunday service at an Irish Catholic church which, right before his eyes, became Spanish-speaking in the early 1960s, with sermons delivered in broken Spanish by Irish priests. The names Mary and Joseph became Maria and Jose, for instance. No matter the language, the result was comical: young Oscar, as he reports in his memoir, falls asleep while his mother, combating disrespect in that holy temple, nearly succumbs to sleep herself.

In this novel, arguably his most pleasurable, Hijuelos sets out to present a story which, to a small degree, involves himself. He is Cuban-American—true. But also, in the blood lineage passed down to him, Irish Celtic—or so his memoir insinuates. In his childhood, he was fair-skinned and blond, *rubio* in Spanish. When he travelled to Cuba with his mother and older brother, he was bounced on the knees of his aunties and uncles, hugged repeatedly, offered sweets, and observed from a distance. His mother was Cuban, his father Cuban. But this blond boy with curls and light skin? The relatives were forced to wonder, *Is this what happens when you go to the United States? You become blond?*

I'm a writer who knows a thing or two about writers—I never invite more than two into my house at any given time. Hijuelos begins *Thoughts without Cigarettes* with the phrase, "Pretend it's sometime in 1956 or 1957 . . ." Now here's a clue about writing fiction if there ever was one: fiction is all about pretending. Acknowledging the beauty of this realization, I offer my own conjecture as well. Let's pretend that Hijuelos started *The Fourteen Sisters of Emilio Montez O'Brien* with the thought of exploring one dimension of his personal life: he's Cuban American, he's Irish American somewhere inside, he's a mix of every lovemaking over the centuries. Hijuelos is at his desk, chuckling to himself. To get started, he bites his pencil for creative nourishment. "Let me see," he says aloud. "What I can do with this?"

Hermano, I see what you have done.

You have written a masterpiece.

ALL I REALLY NEED TO KNOW, I LEARNED IN KINDERGARTEN

By Robert Fulghum

THIS FOLKY 2004 BESTSELLER HAD READERS chuckling in all time zones. It was comfort food for the soul, a simple dish with chunks of edible advice. Fulghum got my attention. When the book came out, I read it, enjoyed it, and suggested it to others at the church I attended at the time.

Still, always a still.

Unlike the author, I didn't learn crap in kindergarten—except not to put crayons up your nostrils. A blue one in the left hole, a yellow one in the right—a pretty picture, I'm sure, and a medical emergency if I had tripped and driven them like nails into my frontal lobe. Think of the rainbow that would have played on the back of my brain! The next autumn, I skipped two doors down into first grade. So, here's a story that wouldn't appear in Fulghum's book. Listen up, followers.

How was it possible for me to anger my first-grade teacher, Miss Yamamoto? Still, one day she turned as violent as a tornado, with a scolding wind howling from her mouth. She yanked my right arm and began to haul me to the front of the class. I did my best to slow our wiggly scuffle up the aisle. I grabbed the edge of a desk, but she pried my fingers loose. I grabbed another desk, and again she unbuckled my fingers. I cried for her to stop and dragged my shoes, thus drawing black marks on the wooden floor. At the front, she lifted me up then swiftly turned me around to face my classmates, all twenty or so, some of whom I liked very much, like my best friend Darrell, and the ponytailed girl I'd chosen as my girlfriend. She had lost her front baby teeth the week before, and her smile was precious.

Miss Yamamoto was the nicest teacher in the whole world— So tall, so pretty! Once a week she honored one student with the

"Seal of Approval" for the tidiest desk. The seal was a stuffed seal, black and white with a red bowtie—and fuzzy. Every Friday after lunch, we rushed into the classroom and excitedly lifted the tops of our desks to see if we had earned the seal. The lucky winner would hug the seal and pet its fuzzy head. The winner would also get a piece of candy.

Such a sloppy boy, I always glared with jealousy. I yearned to spit on the winners and step on their shoes. Push them? Yeah, push them, too. I never got the Seal of Approval, which, by springtime, had been hugged to death. After the bowtie fell off, it resembled a rat. My best friend got it, and my girlfriend got it, and a stupid boy on our block got it. Why wasn't the Seal of Approval ever mine? I arranged my books nicely, one book facing this way, the other that way, and blew all the eraser rubbings from the tub of my metal desk. Was my fingerpainted artwork warped from my erratic rubbing? Were my pencils dull and tooth-marked?

Miss Yamamoto, did I press the button that sparked anger? At the front of the class, you shook me, held my struggling arms, and yelled at me to stop squirming! Then, breathing hard, you let me go, brushed your hair behind your ears, and asked, "How many want Gary to go to the principal's office?" I stood open-mouthed as I watched the entire class raise their hands. I looked at Darrell with his hand up, then lowered halfway, and then up again. And my girlfriend? Her hand was among the first, as if she knew the answer before the question had been asked. Her hand was way up, her fingers even wiggling.

Out the door I went. This was before recess, this was before lunch, on a Friday, the day the Seal of Approval would be awarded. I walked myself down the hallway, where I stopped at a water fountain that offered only a dribble. I continued down the hallway. I wasn't unfamiliar with the routine. I sat in the office and placed my hands in my lap. I swung my legs slowly at first and then fast and high, until the secretary behind her fortress of a desk told me to knock it off.

Then I remembered what I had done: I had torn a page from a picture book. I stood up and took the torn page from *Green Eggs and Ham* out of my back pocket. I looked at it. It meant nothing to me, just another page in my big book of childhood mistakes. The week before, I'd thrown mud at a girl. The week before that, my error had involved a kickball—that's right, I kicked it over the fence when the stupid idiot on third base hadn't scored when he got the chance.

I never got that Seal of Approval in all of first grade, and, on the literary scene, I don't expect it to happen now. To hell with that ugly thing anyway, to hell with a lot of things. Just last week, during a radio interview, the reporter shook me. She was reading the list of my ten favorite writers on my website and asked why not one black writer was included. Was I going to stand in front of the class again without defending myself? I kicked that question over the fence and the arguing began.

Mr. Fulghum, you were a quick learner in kindergarten. Even for me, a slow learner, what I learned then stays with me to this day. Nostrils are no place to put your crayons.

SHAKESPEARE QUOTATIONS

Compiled by Jane Armstrong

I WAS FULL OF SELF-DOUBT ONE MORNING, self-doubt, two donuts and a cup of so-so coffee. I needed a change from padding about the house in my pee slippers. What I needed was a deeper education, where I could open the top of my head and throw in a lot of books. I planned to re-read *The Discoverers*, by Daniel Boorstin, the late and possibly still popular historian, and to reset my intellectual goals by encouraging my brain cells to get their act together. In this state, meaning sober, I intend to hitch up my pants and think deeply about prehistoric matters, like when my distant relative, the Neanderthal man, foraged along the Danube, plodding the muddy earth in an early version of Birkenstocks. I had every belief that education provides novel ways of looking at things. Education leads to jobs and job creation—O, the stimulation of a steady job and a monthly check with ghastly governmental deductions.

Fortified with direction, I meant to study like a Biblical scholar and brush up on the cradle of civilization. The erudition I anticipated called for a brow-furrowed interest in myths, cosmetology—I mean, cosmology—the mysterious source of the Nile, the Euphrates River and Fertile Crescent, algebra as founded by Persian eggheads, contraptions devised by Archimedes, Stonehenge and its worshippers, and stargazing astronomy.

Education! I scolded myself. *Viejo*, try to get smart!

London Town appeared before me, the Bard walking in the shadow of bad rumors. What do I mean by rumors? Some argued that Shakespeare, pen-pusher with a doily-like collar, forehead scrubbed bald from creative worry, pointed nose sniffing for both highbrow and low . . . must have had help from others. He couldn't have written all those plays and sonnets, one brilliant work after another, with inexhaustible genius and commercial sense.

I dispute this rumor. I picture Shakespeare straining to write in a pub lit by candlelight, on a chair backstage of the Globe

Theatre, or in rooms smelly with floors layered with wet hay. I see him in his abode, indifferent to the stink of his urine in the corner pail. His quill busily scratches out lines on parchment. The ink is dark, and his fingers hurt from the pressure of holding a quill, his writing instrument. I see the master sidestepping beggars, thieves and yokels, not in the least pained at the sight of a hen fluttering on a chopping block. Unlike me, he had somewhere to go and something to do. He had to make his living solely from his wits.

Some scholars attribute much of Shakespeare's work to Francis Bacon, while others suggest that Christopher Marlowe came to the rescue. A fellow at Oxford argued that Sir Walter Raleigh penned Shakespeare's later works and that maybe, just maybe, the Countess of Pembroke was involved. I have heard it argued that Queen Elizabeth was the playwright of the Histories. Not true, of course. But, like Shakespeare, she was a wit, both on and off her throne. I recall a lady-in-waiting scolding, "Queen, your hands are so filthy!" Elizabeth might have turned her hands over for a quick inspection. That detail has been lost, but her retort is recorded: "You think my hands are filthy, you should see my feet!"

All the world's a stage, but some scholars should jump off it and go home for tea and a biscuit. Shakespeare was a genius who wrote his plays and verse. He also produced, bankrolled, and, in a pinch, played minor characters. He lived, loved, and died, but his indisputable masterpieces survive.

On the spot, I decided to memorize some Shakespeare quotations. I did this alone with my cat listening. I perfumed the air with Shakespearean couplets and whole stanzas. *Memorize something great*, I told myself, memorize before it's too late.

Later that evening, dressed in one of the Japanese robes I put on when I mean business, I gently prodded my wife to the couch and asked her to sit, to get comfy, to expect an oratory display that would surprise and please. The cat jumped into her lap.

I began with,

> *All the world's a stage*
> *And all the men and women are merely players.*
> *They have their exits and entrances . . ."*

She heard,

> "All aboard, the stagecoach
> And all the hens and women are barely slayers.
> They have their fixits and mentions . . ."

I read,

> *"What's mine is yours, and what's yours is mine."*

She heard,

> "What! Your collapsing mind!"

I read,

> *"Love is blind . . ."*

She heard,

> "Three-Day Blinds . . ."

I read,

> *"But soft, what light through yonder window breaks.*
> *It is the east and Juliet is the sun."*

She heard,

> "But saw, what kite threw yonder windshield crates.
> It is the feast and Julius has the runs!"

I read,

> *"Too famous to live long."*

She heard,

> "Too famished for tongs."

I read

"O you gods!
Why do you make us love your goodly gifts
And snatch them straight away?"

She heard,

"O you frogs!
Why do you fake love you crips
And snatch them from layaway?"

As if speaking in tongues, I recited sixteen other quotations. Then I remembered the so-so film of years ago and the phrase, "Truth is like poetry . . . and you know everyone hates poetry."

I asked what she thought of my recital.

She responded, "You were mumbling."

"Mumbling," I repeated. "Like Bob Dylan singing?"

She nodded. Then she petted the cat's head and quoted the Bard clear as a bell, "Wives may be merry and yet honest too." She touched a new necklace that sparkled between her breasts. "It didn't cost as much as you think."

UNLIKELY FRIENDSHIPS

By Jennifer S. Holland

I APPRECIATE BOOKS DESIGNED WITH LARGE typeface. This is such a book. The typeface on the back cover resembles the lettering on billboards. For instance, the word "Animals" is nearly an inch tall, and in a sturdy font, like rhino legs. This leads me to view this 2011 bestseller as reading material for older people with poor eyesight, wobbly hands struggling to turn the pages. This is a tender book, heartwarming as *Old Yeller* is heartwarming, a Noah's ark of animals presented in unexpected pairs, all worth petting. It's OK to weep over each of these forty-plus entries. One blurb says, "We discover how compassion and empathy smoothly cross species borders."

Am I hoodwinked here? I scratch my dome and think. No doubt about it, this book was meant for people who will easily grow weepy over the stories of abandoned piglets. I scratch my head some more, think some more. Some light is thrown up on the back of my brain, a glow that you might get from a dim flashlight. Then the light brightens, becomes like a floodlight for construction workers on a scaffolding at night.

I clear my throat, sit up. Coins fall from my pocket—I'll pick them later. I have something important to say before I forget. I know you, followers. Most of you are boomers with reading glasses in every room. Many of you benefit from Social Security, like me, like my wife, like the neighbors to my left and right.

"Real friendships have no bounds," says the copy on the inside flap, and here is a maxim that we shouldn't debate, so live with it, OK? Friendships can be established even among creatures outside their own species, animals from all points of the globe, animals that swing in trees, wing about the sky, swim upstream to get home, burrow in the dark earth, even some that may, under different circumstances, be considered for the barbecue grill. But let's not think about that—shame on us as we spread salmon paste on a cracker.

Let's make a few visits. On a riverbank in India, a leopard buddies up to a cow, yet the cow is not taken down by a pair of sharp claws. In Brooklyn, an iguana and a couple of house cats chow down from the same bowl. In Texas, a pit bull, a Siamese cat, and a few chicks hang out in bed. A white rhino and a billy goat roam a nature reserve in South Africa. In fractured Washington, D.C., a Democrat (donkey) plays golf with a Republican (elephant), each kicking the ball along to get the game over with. Then off to the clubhouse where they share a bowl of pretzels and mugs of beer, photos of family life, an off-color joke or two, then write off the occasion as a business expense.

Of course, no Democrats or Republicans appear in this politically neutral book. This is a story that's far more noble. It's the sort of book that evokes the melodic sounds of a river in the background, wind in a stand of eucalyptus, birds chirping, the roar of a lion in the distance. Here's a story that takes us back to 1984. In California, Koko the gorilla was taught sign language. Moreover, she was read to as a toddler might be read to. Her favorite books? *The Three Little Kittens* and *Puss in Boots*. With a birthday approaching, Koko was asked what she wanted. She ran a finger under her nose, a sign for whiskers, a clue that she wished for a cat. She had stuffed toys, possibly a stuffed cat among them, but for her birthday she begged for a live kitten that meowed and pranced. And so it happened, the gift was delivered. Koko received a shelter kitten. The 240-pound gorilla was completely smitten and rolled around her cage to demonstrate her joy. She loved her new friend, named Ball. Eventually the most horrible thing occurred: the kitten was run over by a car.

Man, why did I mention the kitten's death—a mood killer. Let me return us to a better place and introduce you to another unlikely pairing: a nearsighted deer and a poodle—now that sounds like the start of a joke. Oh, and who do we have stepping off the ark next? The dachshund and the piglet? The hippopotamus and the pygmy goat? The Asiatic black bear and the black cat? The snake and the hamster? The macaque and the dove? The rat and the cat? Gary Soto and Carolyn Sadako Oda? A few consider this pairing, this marriage of fifty years, as unlikely as the skunk bedding down with the world's most adorable creature, the panda.

How about the golden retriever named Chino and the koi who went by Falstaff? I will flesh out their relationship. First, Chino was not a friendly pooch. He went on walks with his people but never horsed around with other dogs in the park. His tail was not the tail of a dog running in circles. He did not roll over in expectation of being petted. Barking for treats—like, hell no. He was too dignified to suck up to people. And forget his licking your hand or affectionally poking his nose into your crotch. Falstaff lived with another koi, unnamed, in the backyard pond. Can't say that Falstaff was friendly with the other fish—to my mind, the pair of koi were Zen-like creatures, a softening effect in the garden pond. But religion was not part of the fish's upbringing. They were just lovely ornaments, like live earrings.

We know that dogs respond to their names, but koi? Don't think so. They're exotic, beautifully exotic, and get by with three or four molecules that work as a fish's thinking cap. It's like how I am some days when I get by with three or four neurons that I call a brain. My wife will yell from her sewing room, "Gary, I need your help!" I'll look up and consider my wife's words. *It's me, she wants*, I'll tell myself, pointing at my belly. I'll sit up in the comfy armchair and toss whatever I'm reading aside. But when the landline rings and the voice on the other end says, "Gary! You old bag of bones," I'm like the koi, *muy* silent, hiding beneath a metaphorical lily pad. (Readers, I never answer my phone, for the caller is always from the past—and the past involves people I don't want to see anymore.)

Did I veer off subject? Let us return to my narrative. The golden retriever and the koi became infatuated with each other, even though they live in different elements, which doesn't allow them to cuddle. Their approach to friendship? They anticipate each other's daily arrival, then look at each other, often touching each other's noses.

And what do we learn here, if learning has anything to do with books? The author, Jennifer S. Holland, suggests that animals have empathy and feelings. You can see love in their eyes, she says. And like us humans, they have needs. If a koi offers up a bubble that snaps on the surface of the water, what of it? Got to wonder what's inside that bubble, what is being communicated. We humans communicate by speech, song, smiles, frowns, and hand gestures (usually flipping off each other while trucking down the road). If you're, say, a deer or possum, creatures of the semi-wild, you don't want to be physically close to people. But domestic animals have learned to snuggle up to humans. Dogs yearn to be petted and taken on walks, with tennis balls in their chops. Cats expect the warmth of central heating. Imagine the tenderness of a monkey sitting on top of your head—that sort of thing.

I sit up and look around, curious about the clunking noise from downstairs. I push myself up, walk down the hallway and, lightly touching the handrail, descend to the basement level of our house, a haven when the occasional heatwave overwhelms us. I stop, turn around and listen—clunking from the furnace room. I open the door and swipe at the light switch. There sits a robot-like furnace insulated in silvery foil and—what's this?

I take a step back. It's my cat with blood on his whiskers and a large rat caught in a trap. The cat's eyes are wildly shiny, the rat's eyes murky with clouds. This is not a scene from *Unlikely Friendships*; no, this is possibly an outtake from a Korean horror film.

Sorry, I think. *Sorry, Mousey, for your troubles.*

I close the door to let them continue sorting out their relationship. The way I see it, it's hard to choose friendship if what's inside your friend tastes really, really good.

PORTABLE MAGIC, A HISTORY OF BOOKS AND THEIR READERS

By Emma Smith

WHAT'S THIS, A RIVAL? AND WRITTEN BY A SCHOLAR who holds an appointment at Oxford? I feel voiceless as a rooster who has lost his crow. I reflect, scratch my chin, reflect some more. It's only 1:34 Pacific Standard Time, four hours and a few meaningless minutes before I can uncap a beer. I close my eyes and imagine Professor Smith's life. Is she wetting her whistle at this moment? A glass of Chablis, perhaps? Sherry? I imagine the characters in Downton Abbey, Lord-This and Lady-That, holding thimble-size sherry glasses. But I have it all wrong, I realize. Smith is in a different time zone and across the pond. She must be asleep by now, her academic gown and mortarboard waiting on a chair for the morning.

I bought *Portable Magic* before I became an influencer and started to make public statements that turned heads in Idaho and Montana. During those months I glanced at this book, picked it up, put it back down, read some, and confessed to my inner self, Man, Professor Smith is hecka smart. She has a comfortable voice in explaining the history of books. She doesn't speak down to us jobless yokels. Still, she employs what is called "academic framing," which gives structure to her theories. Also, her book has an index, and mine, in manuscript form, doesn't. Followers, let me explain things. An index appears in the back of a scholarly book and references the subjects discussed within its pages. Let me visit an example from Professor's Smith index:

Hardy, Thomas: "The Convergence of the Twain," 112; *Jude the Obscure*, 138; *Tess of the d'Urbervilles*, 9–10

My index, with massive inaccuracies, would include the following:

St. Pauli Girl, 3, 5, 9, 17, 37, 67 87, 17, 8, 79, 3

I offer another example from Professor's Smith's book:
  Eliot, George, *Middlemarch*, 63, 69

And another example from mine:
  Tex-Mex poet talking shit, 75; vomiting on azalea bush, 76

Dr. Smith also uses sources that are beyond my local jurisdiction. For instance, in researching her subject, she used the Morgan Library New York, the New York Public Library, the British Library, the Bodleian Library, the Ransom Center in Austin, Texas, the Cambridge University Library, and other places of higher learning. Smart of her to figure out how to connect online and keep all her passwords filed away in her head. In writing my reviews, I occasionally scanned my library card at the self-checkout table at the public library or perused the bookshelves in our hallway. Occasionally, when I pulled out a poetry book from the 1980s, the photo of the poet sported a beard of dust. And the poet was often dead or, like the Picts, had disappeared, perhaps down the hallway of a state college.

Professor Smith acknowledges help from others by providing a generous list at the end of the book. She names sixty-eight individuals, many of whom, I suspect, are scholars, book collectors, librarians, educated friends, proofreaders, bookbinders, and writers themselves. She did move a mountain of words that became beautifully sloping sentences, each like a ski run; but still, I had to wonder if she needed all that help. Me? I acknowledge my wife, Carolyn, and the cat, name withheld because of confidentiality. The furry guy's repeated feedback? Meow.

The title of *Portable Magic* comes from Stephen King, who purportedly wrote in an article that books have "a uniquely portable magic." The title of my book comes from hugging an armful of empties while taking them to my recycling bin on the side of the house. I hug them like friends, like buddies. I toss them, one by one, and shout a hearty, "Hey, let's do it again tomorrow tonight!"

There's so much that's memorable in Professor Smith's writing if you are, in fact, a reader who likes to remember things.

For me, remembering is overrated, unless, of course, you're an airline pilot and need to know your way around the buttons on the dash. Memory sounds like a human trait worth embracing. However, I'm going to side with moment. For me, Moment (the present) towers over Memory (the past).

Smith writes witty prose with enough levity that I would very much like to invite her over for a drink. She balances her discoveries with seriousness, with humor, with conclusions that we trust. She knows her business. She writes, for instance, "Acknowledging bookhood demands that we resist the tendency to idealize them. Books are wonderful, challenging, transporting—but sometimes also sickening, disturbing, enraging."

Doesn't "sickening, disturbing, enraging" sound like our current politics? Sorry, I'm off the subject. Let's just look at the word *bookhood*. Followers, are you confused by this word? Professor Smith has an explanation. Bookhood is what you're doing when you're holding a book in your hands, possibly one of my titles, a hardback if possible. You're in the "hood" or *el barrio* or a gated community with a private pool. Bookhood means wherever you turn—living room, bedroom, bathroom, study (if you're lucky enough to have one), or hallway—you encounter something to read.

Books challenge us. (Read her introduction twice, a challenge I hope you gladly accept.) I also find that books "transport," sometimes bumpily, and at a reasonable cost. But as for Dr. Smith's descriptor "wonderful," I'm not sure. Some highly praised—and honored—books are not that good. My wife was happy a few days ago, then woke up grumpy because I had gotten her a novel about Japanese robots—by an author who won a Nobel Prize (in literature, not science). Her morning face said, Stinko birthday present, before a cup of coffee was inside her and she was fully awake.

Emma Smith, professor and scholar, is on our side, people. Her area of studies is Shakespeare and, like one of the Bard's characters, she's up on the stage delivering lines meant to embrace bookhood and make us momentarily smarter.

I'll drink to that.

THE ANCIENT MINSTREL
By Jim Harrison

LET'S SAY THAT HARRISON IS A BETTER PROSE
stylist than Charles Bukowski, but both are geniuses whose books
put readers in happy moods. Both were drinkers, it has been
verified, and both were irreverent to all matters literary—though
Harrison did teach, win awards, make the bestseller list, and
encounter poets and writers climbing up the ladder to find
nothing at the top.

This influencer, sober after a weekend of silliness, requires
laughter. This Monday I received a photocopied rejection from
a Texas journal. Rumor has it that the editor wears a bowtie,
while his leather-skinned compadres in the English department—
the ones I would like—wear metaphorical toilet seats around their
necks. Now what do I mean by that toilet-seat thing? Toil with
it, followers. Use your thinking caps. While you're at it, befriend
some poets and buy them drinks and bags of peanuts.

I'm done sobbing. I'm here to say that Harrison, a personal
favorite, was master of two genres, poetry and prose, a literary
mixture to my liking. He also wrote screenplays and met movie stars.
Now I address one of his books. This novella, *The Ancient Minstrel,*
is autobiographical. How do I know this? He says in the first
sentence, *"Some years ago when I was verging on sixty years and feeling
poignantly the threat of death I actually said to myself, 'Time to write
a memoir'"* [his italics, not mine].

But is this *really* a memoir? He claims it is. Some of it sounds
like Harrison, with a heart that beats part of the year in Montana
and then part of the time in the southwest (Arizona, I believe).
He does refer to our narrator in the third person, as if he separated
his own self slightly from this vision of himself (in childhood,
Harrison suffered an eye injury, forcing him to go through life
with one all-seeing eyeball). So, when our narrator says, "he did
this" or "he did that," you might be right in judging that you're
reading fiction. Perhaps Harrison is pulling the strings of literary

puppetry and is also pulling our leg. Let's say that 60 percent of this novella is true to life—that's good enough to size up the man and his personal literary ambitions, his open attraction to Hollywood money, his teaching career, his European jaunts, his taste for beer and chasers, his woodsman-like character, his rod and reel, his one bulging eye on unattainable girls in miniskirts, his birdwatching, and his occasional pigheadedness in marriage. In fact, your influencer is taking us right to page 53 and the reference to pigs, those bacon strips of the future. In the previous pages, the narrator inexplicitly buys a mothering pig. He is giddy for this pig, blessed with the name Darling. He's middle-aged, full of doubt about this and that, and decides to search for meaning by building a pen, ordering a trough, and buying foodstuff for the promised piglets. *Presto*, the mothering pig soon has six or seven critters on her teats. He names three newborns and ignores naming the others.

One afternoon, after a phone call with a New York editor (Harrison elevates this literary posturing with hints of self-importance; Bukowski doesn't), he goes outside to discover Shirley, one of the piglets and the runt of the litter, gone. He whistles for his dog, Mary. He's mightily perturbed by the absence of Shirley, who an hour ago was basking in mud. It's time to hunt for his baby. He deputizes Mary, a black cocker spaniel. The two hurry to the rescue.

I must pause my commentary here, followers. Got to sit up and look snappy. My wife has come into the living room. She has some sort of stitchery in her hand and a couple of pins in her mouth. She removes the pins and glares at me—yes, followers, glares at little ole me. We had yet another argument about whether the Easter Islands are located north or south of the equator. A worthy debate in our latter years.

I ask my wife, "Am I smart?"

She answers, "Sometimes."

I ponder the images on my rain-stained ceiling—has Jesus been crying through our insulation? Then I level my attention on my dear wife. "Am I smart right now?"

After a few seconds of silence, she answers frostily, "You're dumb as boards."

A few seconds click away from life. I look out the picture window, then smile at my wife. Snarky me, I ask, "Those boards, would they be pine or oak?"

The floor creaks, the wind pushes against the window. "Balsa wood," she replies. "Very light stuff."

She leaves the room, taking away all hope of a decent dinner. I chuckle to the very lonely poet that dwells inside my soul. My wife speaks the truth and so does Harrison, though he fibs here and there. He writes about piglets and sides with the runt which—this is terrible news, followers—is squished to death when the mothering pig rolls over her. Yes, Shirley, the rescued runt is fuckin' dead!

I could hack off a few hours more describing this wonderful testimony of a writer's life. But I'm not in the mood, followers, and not because of my wife's view of me as balsa wood, weightless and easy to crumble. No, it's because my thoughts return to the novella and the saddest confession ever: "It was hard to get enough money for a drink."

This would not be during his college years. All of us MFA students had a tough time pulling together dimes and quarters for cheap grog. No, this was when he was a nearly established writer. He might have shaken his beer for foam, licked the lip of the bottle, put an ear to its mouth for some message of hope, maybe added a little water to the bottle and pretended to be drinking. Who knows? But, for me, a writer's soul is in the tender line, "It was hard to get enough money for a drink."

Why did I begin this review by mentioning Harrison and Bukowski, both geniuses, in the same breath? After all, I haven't said much else about Bukowski. Let me supply the answer. Because they look alike, these literary twins, and both wrote books that wavered between human despair and utter joy for life—crazy, crazy, crazy. I love both writers, but from a distance. Again, their books put readers in good moods, but the authors themselves are no longer present. I sigh at this truth; both are gone, though remembered in this household. They should get postage stamps with their images front and center. They should—but those who vote on such matters won't raise a hand in their favor. Me, I would have raised a hand, just like I do at my local dive, The Hotsy Totsy. "Henry!" I sing to the bartender. *"The same for Harrison and Bukowski. And a St. Pauli Girl for me"* [my use of italics].

FOLK WISDOMS OF MEXICO
Translated by Jeff M. Sellers

YOUR INFLUENCER KNOWS SCHOOLS. LET ME EXPLAIN.

Decades ago, I was invited to give a presentation of my writings for young people at an elementary school in the San Joaquin Valley. I knew that most of the students would be Mexican or Mexican-American. What should I do? I told myself. I had a hunch that they might like to view my collection of Mexican crafts. I was right on this account. I displayed my carved wooden animals, my clay bells, a few articles of embroidered clothing from Oaxaca, some clay and tin whistles, a tray of *milagros*, my *sarape* woven by Zacharias Ruiz of Teotitlán del Valle, and just about everything in my household that sparkled and was imbued with cultural beauty. I even displayed a pair of *aretes*—earrings—on a white cloth. The children enjoyed them, turning them over in their hands. Not one thing broke.

In one class period I brought out a typed and photocopied list of proverbs and riddles. My intention was to keep the children guessing and wondering with curiosity at things that are Mexican. The proverbs and riddles were in Spanish with English translations. So, I stood up in front of the class with the answers in my hands, asking, "OK, who can answer why the egg went blind?" I imagined that I would baffle and tease them, but I was wrong. Hands shot up like a tribe of spears and pained looks saying "Call on me! Call on me!" squinched up their faces. I was the one who was baffled. The book from which I had drawn the riddles was an obscure text from the Chicano Studies Library at Cal Berkeley, certainly not readily accessible to the public, let alone these children who lived far from Berkeley. How could these *esquincles* know that it was the farmer who had poked the eyes out of his two eggs at breakfast? Right then I understood who these kids were: rural children from Mexican families who had been hearing a litany of proverbs since birth. The game was quickly over for me. Suddenly the tables were turned: these fourth graders were asking me if I could answer some riddles that they knew. I was terrifically embarrassed because I couldn't answer even one in my *pocho* Spanish. Surely, I thought, there must be a proverb about the bigshot teacher who is taught a good lesson by students with grass stains on their knees.

The Mexican proverb is the verbal property of common people. It is a condensed saying, some pithy remark from a man leaning on his plow or a woman with her elbows up on a table as she listens to the *chisme*—gossip—of a neighbor. The Mexican proverb may inform and advise, or it may offer an arguable point to life. It is amusement and it is wisdom itself. It is the snappy scolding of a naughty child. It is the soothing remedy to loss and the loss of hope. It is the logic of unrequited love and the finger-wagging judgement on greed and gluttony. It is a warning and a conclusion. It is the unwritten literature and philosophy of the poor, particularly rural folk. While the wealthy and educated have Carlos Fuentes and Octavio Paz, the man or woman on the street has songs, limericks, folklore, *chisme*, and proverbs such as "*Quien mas mira menos ve*" (The more one looks, the less one sees). So much for focused and mind-tiring education, this proverb seems to conclude.

Most Mexican proverbs have been passed down from generation to generation with only a sign of changes. They are frequently regional yet universal in appeal. That they have European roots is certain, and that they have been shared verbally instead of in books is also certain. Mexican proverbs may not be as old as rock, but they are at least as old as the largest trees in the *zocalos* of rural towns. They share the qualities of proverbs from other cultures: they are sharp and distilled truths.

Proverbs reunite the listener with his or her ancestors. They bear witness to the ancient human foibles that continue to plague us to this day. It takes only a kitchen table, or two chairs situated under a mulberry tree, to hear a chattering of rural history summed up with an appropriate proverb. If you are like me, the grandson of *una abuela* who came to the United States at the end of the Mexican revolution, you might hear a story from a seventy-two-year-old woman, who heard it from her grandmother Graciela Treviño, who heard it first from her *tia*, the aunt who was widowed for no more than two years before taking up with that rake Don José López, who was a good man in the end and, *pues*, responsible for digging a well in San Pedro Piedra Gorda, Zacatecas—or so the history might have it between sips of coffee. In turn, proverbs as well as tales live through the passing of a day and not in the turning of a page.

The farther north Mexicans have trudged into the United States, the fewer proverbs one hears in conversation. There may be fewer occasions to use them in these new surroundings or fewer people to appreciate their clever cleverness. They begin to disappear within one generation, along with the use of Spanish, and are replaced with less clever phrasings. Children perk up more to television jingles and words from pop songs than they do to proverbs, Mexican or otherwise. They know athletes and brand names. In short, the world for them is so visual that their verbal dexterity is limited to the momentary zing of commercials and advertisements.

So, what am I getting at? A proverb to leave you with.

A poet once arrived in a rural town in the San Joaquin Valley, and didn't know a damn thing.

REMINISCENCES
OF A STUDENT'S LIFE
By Jane Ellen Harrison

EARLIER I REPORTED THAT MY BELOVED FIRST-GRADE
teacher Miss Yamamoto once yanked me to the front of the class
and asked, "How many want Gary to go to the principal's office?"
Arms shot up like spears, including both arms of my best friend
Darrell. I was voted out of the class. On that day I received a mild
warning from the principal and then was excused to return to class.
But I didn't return to class. I walked off the school grounds and
went up an alley where I drummed wildly on an oil drum—that is,
until a dog, boosted up by a greasy-haired biker type, peered over
the fence and growled at me.

What does the above paragraph have to do with scholar
Harrison's eighty-four-page memoir? Not sure, followers, but stay
with me. Let me just say Harrison, unknown these days, went
about her days with a brilliant mind. Her childhood in Yorkshire
was bucolic, with a devoted dog named Moscow and little wooden
blocks that she used to taste, a memory that stayed with her. She
was the daughter of a timber merchant (her mother died soon
after her birth). A beauty? The introduction says that she posed for
Pre-Raphaelite painters. Educated at home by governesses, she was
self-propelled by early curiosities, the quietness of her surroundings, and books, lots of books. She attended church: cold shadows
on stone walls, and coldness from the Yorkshire villagers (they
didn't take to outsiders, including the clergy who were sometimes
rotated into the parish from other parts of Great Britain). She had
an ear for Yorkshire speech and its rural cadence. Here's an example:
"Yer'll maybe be lawnly wi'out Missie, happens yer'd fancy a dook
fer yer dinner."

I wish I had grown up with such verbal gift.

At age twenty-four, Harrison entered Newnham College for
Women at Cambridge. The year was 1874. Ms. Harrison was ahead

of her time. Her fields of study included Greek antiquities, Russian history and society, art, archeology, and anthropology. When asked by Prime Minster William Gladstone her favorite Greek writer, she at first answered Homer, then revised her answer. No, she told the prime minister, it's Euripides.

Brilliant, so brilliant. I smile at this sentence on page 11: "My father was incapable of forming a [religious] conviction, but I think he really would have sympathized with the eminent statesman [Gladstone, I presume] who had 'a great respect for religion as long as it didn't interfere with a gentleman's private life!'"

That's my position, too. Religion can be such a stifler.

Harrison was not easily swayed by convention. She befriended priests and even a bishop, who once placed a hand on the top of her head and blessed her talents as an organist (she did play the organ, but only as a pastime). Of her beliefs, she said: "the apparatus of religion interested me. I followed the prayers in Latin, the lessons in German, and the Gospel in Greek."

Latin, German, and Greek! Add French, Russian, and some Hebrew, along with the brain power to discuss serious subjects from all angles. She could "read" the scenes displayed on ancient Greek vases, for instance, and see the stories present in other works of art. Mind you, she lived during a time when women enrolled at Cambridge or Oxford couldn't earn a degree. They had to settle for a certificate. (Oxford changed the policy in the 1920s and Cambridge, her university, after World War II).

Harrison enjoyed her curiosity, developed opinions on all things serious, and searched out people who liked what she liked. Her prose style (in this book, at least) was entertaining and her public lectures well organized and attended.

Now I've figured out why I'm so curious about this slender book. First, it was published by Hogarth Press, the press founded by Virginia and Leonard Woolf—what literary heritage! Second, here is a person who recognized her purpose, at least partly because her childhood was the "old-fashioned" kind, a childhood that allowed her to read and think without much interruption. Her father was a shy and encouraging figure, her stepmother a religious evangelical but not a mean sort. In adulthood, her intellectual interests ranged widely, but she kept returning to Greek mythology. A good evening for her? Tea and discussion with like-minded friends about Athenian gravestones.

Harrison, a successful public lecturer, also taught at Cambridge. She was a curious soul, though not physically brave. In childhood, she feared horses, for instance. In her thirties and forties, she lived in London and, no surprise, played roles in Greek tragedies staged in the homes of friends and acquaintances. She even encouraged Isadora Duncan to consider Greek material—which Duncan did.

Harrison was voluble, they say, self-confident even among the intellectual elite. Prime Minister Herbert Asquith said she was the most "distinguished woman scholar in (the use of) the word." She made trips abroad—to France, Russia, and the United States—but mostly remained in Great Britain. "By what miracle did I escape marriage I do know not," she wrote, "for all my life I fell in love." When her memoir was published, in 1925, she was living with a woman thirty-seven years younger than she. A scholarly romantic, a predecessor to, say, the art critic and novelist Anita Brookner. Ms. Brookner never married either.

Here's where I bring myself into Harrison's life story. There are days, followers, when I believe I could have been like Harrison, studious and worldly. I have loads of books, vision, and an eye for interpretation—what that rain-stained ceiling is presently telling me, for instance, I keep private. Would Harrison have fallen in love with me? She says that she was easily capable of love. The answer is in the next paragraph—a sloppy transition, yes, but I'm no Antia Brookner.

I wish the eminent scholar, who reassembled a Greek goddess, could have walked down a Fresno alley in 1956 and observed me beating a stick against an oil drum. She might have smiled at my doltish energy. Yes, smiled and placed a hand on her heart. But no, I tell myself, she probably would have sneered at my lack of musical talent and broken the stick over my head, like my mother would have. Her beautiful face would have slowly turned then, to size up the dog and its biker owner. *No Greek myths here,* she would have concluded. She might have observed me for a few more seconds, synthesized the moment's importance, and then, like my entire first-grade class, slowly raised an arm.

A vote to send Gary to that Big Principal in the mythological sky.

CROW: FROM THE LIFE
AND SONGS OF THE CROW
By *Ted Hughes*

I WAS INTRODUCED TO THIS BOOK OF POEMS IN 1973, when my hair was black as Crow, my scream the scream of Crow, my eyes dark as Crow, taking Crow steps with Crow legs and rough knees, Crow beak jabbing for food. Then—as now—I'm not sure what this book is about, other than a mixture of pagan and Christian mythology and one ugly bird determined to survive, as in "Crow had to start searching for something to eat." I was twenty-one years old. The book defined my malnourished college days. I was Crow surviving on watery oatmeal and potatoes, frozen waffles, eggs, chili beans, free oranges, raisins—until from a tree (a bedroom window, in truth) I made out in my beady bird's-eye view a young woman who could feed me. She lived next door and had her own bird-ness: short, very short, she resembled a lovely penguin whenever she came out of the house and bounced down the cement steps. She saw me from my sophomore perch, crackers falling from my mouth. She waved and waved. I flew over to her house and discovered a stocked pantry. The year was 1973. The month, March. The world was no longer a cold place.

Befuddled me, I got off the subject—sorry, so sorry. Let me regroup, followers.

Hughes's poetry was a reverent moment. I bought this book, read it daily, and began to imagine England, with its skies dark with crows. Hughes' poetry was a strange language, a mythic drumming. In Fresno our local bird was the sparrow, the color of gravel, small and without a chirp. I saw myself as a sparrow, not a crow with blood on its beak.

The second poem in the collection is titled "Lineage." Hughes writes,

> In the beginning was Scream
> Who begat Blood
> Who begat Eye
> Who begat Fear
> Who begat Wing
> Who begat Bone
> Who begat Granite

And there's more to come, a whole series of begats, a word unknown to me in my early twenties and one that I have yet to use in public. Totally English, I thought back then, this word that seemed full of power doom. Like the Bible, Crow had authority, a profound cadence, and a creationist take demonstrated by a bird with a vicious brain. The book comes off the shelf now and then to remind me that I'm a creature that eats with a special guest. The guest is named Poetry.

THE POETRY OF PABLO NERUDA
By Pablo Neruda

WHEN I RETURNED HOME FROM DOING NOT A whole lot in the world, my wife, a homebody who accomplishes much as a clothes designer, told me that our grandson, Toshi, had asked, "What's Grandpa doing on the cover?"

"The cover of what?" I replied, tossing my jacket onto a dining-room chair. From my pants pocket I brought out a foxtail, the single product of my day out in public. I twirled it between my index finger and thumb, then placed it on an end table. *What did my wife mean?*

"Neruda's book," she answered. She pointed and asked, "What's that?"

"A foxtail." I lifted my left pant leg. "It was in my sock."

My wife's eyes became sharp. I could have come through the door with red roses. But, no, it was a straggly foxtail. Was that the best I could do?

I went to my bookshelf and scanned the titles, repeating under my breath so as not to forget, "Neruda, Neruda, Neruda." My chant slowed to a whisper—there, there was the book, 981 pages of vibrant poetry that I plucked from the shelf. In the cover photo, Neruda stands on the deck of an iron-clad ship, hat tilted smartly, a muffler around his neck, wearing a long woolen coat, and holding in his left hand a package wrapped in newspaper. He is either leaving Chile or returning to Chile. I consider the photo for a few more seconds, doing my own calculations about this juncture in his life. The decade, I suspect, is the 1950s. The great poet was in trouble in his home-land—he must have been leaving Chile. His face, I see, shows no happiness.

To my grandson Toshi, I resemble Neruda. Could this be true? I studied Neruda's image and saw greatness in his features.

I doubt that this quality dwells in my creased face, but I beam at our grandson, a wordsmith at age three. I've got to say that Toshi, a listener to stories such as *Frog and Toad*, is highly verbal and extremely alert. He is the small hand behind a toy dump truck that hauls pebbles from one side of our yard to the other. He wears a bright-lime safety vest sewn by my wife. He likes to go "beep-beep" when the dump truck goes in reverse. In short, he's a perfect toddler. From dirt and weeds, he's building something that will be around for a long time.

Is it possible that, as we age, we begin to look like the writers we admire? For me, it is this Chilean poet. Briefly, I close my eyes, open them. What lucky star boomeranged against my head when I was twenty years old, with an orange in one pocket, an apple in the other? I was a young man with black, black hair, a thin waist, using a pencil sharpened by my own teeth. And those teeth of mine were not human teeth but the teeth of a jaguar. My limbs were not human limbs but the limbs of redwoods that drank their fill from rivers that raced west toward the sea. And the orange and apple in my pocket? They were devoured, the seeds shooting wildly from my mouth—the poetry planted for others—all because of Neruda.

I could have translated more of his poems but didn't—a lapse of judgement. But the Spanish-language part of my brain did translate one poem that was included in *The Poetry of Pablo Neruda*, edited by Ilan Stavans.

House

Maybe this is the house where I lived
When I did not exist, when earth did not exist,
When everything was moon or stone or shadow,
When the motionless lights had yet to rise.

Maybe then this stone was
My house, my windows or my eyes.
It reminds me, this granite rose,
Of something that inhabited me or that I inhabited,
Cave or cosmic head of dreams,
Cup or castle or ship or source of my beginnings.
I touch the rock's tenacious effort,
Its bulwark, beaten in the brine,
And I know that here remain my crevices,
The wrinkled substance that climbed
From the depths of my soul—
I was stone, will become stone. That is why
I touch this stone, and for me it has not died:
It's what I was, what I will be, my rest
From a battle as long as time.

WALDEN

By Henry David Thoreau

I PLACE THE BOOK ON THE ORANGE, UPHOLSTERED ottoman in front of the comfy armchair. Leaning over, I touch its cover, pet it like a cat. I consider the philosopher poet's rumination on his stay in nature. It's contrary to my own inner directive and sudden status as an influencer. If you've come this far with me, you can see for yourself that you're reading a literary comedy. I'm not, in truth, the poet hankering for a beer at the end of the day. A daily bowl of cereal is closer to my character, a third cup of coffee risky business.

In *Walden*, Thoreau "withdraws" from Concord, Massachusetts, and we're all the better for his decision. His account is honest, his viewpoint on survival practical. (In his relative youth, he had observed carpenters at work, farmers, too, and put what he saw to use. Otherwise, he would have frozen to death the first winter, if the mosquitos hadn't drained him of blood first.) Your influencer can be generous in praise, and praise is due here. He is an elegant prose stylist proverbial with his gifts, though not with the thigh-slapping humor of Mark Twain. For me, the Bible comes to mind. Look at this line, which regards his near purchase of a farm: "I never got my fingers burned by actual possession." Such language is poetically alluring. Burned from a blistered palm, burned by failed crops, burned from sun and wind, burned by ownership and a mortgage like a dark shadow over your shoulder, always there.

Thoreau makes his way to a place called Walden, a wooded property owned by Ralph Waldo Emerson, with the intention "to live deep and suck out all the marrow of life." He plans to build a cabin far from the city. Thoreau chooses a life free of daily burdens other than his work of hewing lumber from trees. He considers himself a speculator on ownership. There's humor here, followers.

He sees himself purchasing *this* farm and *that* farm and those farms way yonder. He cultivates an image as "sort of a real estate broker by my friends." He's a big spender in his imagination, though at the time he could only jiggle ten cents in his pocket. We've all done this, I suppose, speculated on Sundays when there are open houses in nearby neighborhoods. We wipe the soles of our shoes, enter bashfully, look but don't touch, and take the flyer that describes the house and termite report. Later we imagine ourselves in that mid-century house we've always wanted. If we ever do purchase that house, we will put out a welcome mat—a mat that says "Welcome."

This is my take, followers, on *Walden*, and Thoreau's subtle manner in encouraging the search for our own Walden and the peace it offers. Thoreau is welcoming us to another kind of life, one off the grid. On this parcel of land, he enjoys a pond and the stream that feeds the pond, trees and the coolness of wind through the trees, a life among birds, deer, and beavers, and—once you have wakened to nature—discernable seasons. He worries for our nation—*Why should the government allow slavery*, for instance.

Thoreau describes existence on a farther shore. He cultivates an inner life while laboring in constructing a cabin. He learns a thing or two about seeds, fish nibbling the surface of the pond, the slant of rain, apples pinched from a neighbor. He hires himself out to a nearby farmer. And yet, I got to wonder whether he was a true laborer. My guess is *not*. But he could dig some, cook for himself, and construct a one-room structure that wouldn't pass muster with the city planners these days. He could grow corn, observe deer tracks, keep a journal, and talk under his breath. As he describes his relationship with a farmer, "[I] took his word for his deed, for I dearly love to talk."

I know a poet who withdrew from life. He got off the grid—phone and computer particularly—and disappeared. That was an extreme exit plan. I like my quiet life, but I wouldn't mind interruptions from the outside world—what's that noise, our mail carrier Kelly approaching the front door? In truth, it's quiet here, the mouse and mouse's bigger cousin, the rat, having moved out. I will occasionally pick up my landline phone to see if it's in working order. It always is. But no one calls. The house creaks and so do I. What I imagined was the mail carrier was just a free newspaper cartwheeling on the walkway.

I'm not rustic. Unlike Thoreau, I wear gloves when I work in the yard. I mist my neck with mosquito repellent. A straw hat shades my eyes. I do have trees in my life, though. If I open the front door, a tall redwood planted in 1952, the year of my birth, shares its coolness with me. Occasionally a neighbor, giraffe tall, comes to hug the tree and departs peeling tears from her eyes. I once patted the tree in friendship, but didn't offer a hug. In fall, the needles from the redwood bury my annuals.

There's no doubting Thoreau's affinity for solitude. Let me display some of his words and phrases: "serenity," "alone," "experiment of this kind," "a lake like this," "renew thyself completely each day," "aurora," "a vast horizon," "small lake," "wooded valley." These pastoral offerings would do well in a Constable oil painting. He writes: "I wanted to live deliberately, to [con]front the essential facts of life." Prior to this experiment, Thoreau worked in his family's pencil factory and, in his spare time, lectured and wrote philosophical prose. An idealist, he was firmly against slavery.

Each paragraph in Chapter 2 of *Walden* is worth rereading. For instance, Thoreau portrays a "crusty" farmer mulling over the departure of a poet who worked the land for a bit. This farmer might have spat, then sized up the poet as a loafer, one who couldn't hold up his end of the bargain. Instead, the poet's time there became "rimes," a literary crop that he turned over and over in his imagination. Perhaps Thoreau is that poet who worked the land, then dusted himself off and returned to Concord to write a national treasure—*Walden*.

I'm neither a Thoreau nor an Emerson. Indeed, I'm not any of the transcendentalists of the mid-1800s. Still, I grasp their intentions. Let's then ask ourselves where we live and what we live for. Specifically, what's the vibe like inside the house, what does the décor say about us? And what is our purpose? We can examine our routines and find out. I don't want to play the know-it-all in the pulpit box. However, if I examine my routines, it's easy to assess my unadventurous self. I talk to my cat each morning. While I ramble, the furry guy often licks his front paws without bothering to look up. This morning, I scolded, "Corky, if you're going to eat a rat, eat all of it! It's impolite to leave his tail and feet at the back door!"

This may be the deepest conversation I'm going to have all day. No one will visit, no one will call. My junk mail often has to do with window washing or duct cleaning. Is this quiet indifference *my* Walden? I sigh at the possibility. Morning is almost over. The coffee has been drunk, the spoon dipped into a bowl of raw oats darkened with raisins, and now here's a book that I haven't visited in years. *Walden* sits on that orange, upholstered ottoman. I touch the cover, pet it. I tell myself that a philosopher poet went into the woods and then came out of the woods, all the wiser. He brought back the scent of nature and solitude, a rarity these days.

HOW DID IT BEGIN?
By Dr. R. & L. Brasch

THIS BOOK DOESN'T INVOLVE THE BIG BANG AND earth's spectacular creation, but the sources of our human customs and superstitions. Got to say that I'm not usually superstitious, though if I have a chance of walking around a ladder or walking under it, I walk around it. Why tempt fate?

What customs and superstitions are explained in this entertaining book? Spilling salt, unlucky number 13, knocking on wood, lucky horseshoes, third time a charm, breaking a mirror, a rabbit's foot for luck, opening an umbrella inside the house, stepping on cracks, the advent of crocodile tears, blue for boys, pink for girls, storks and babies—these sorts of explanations.

Let me slow down here and touch upon the rabbit's foot. An explanation in one concise sentence: the rabbit was looked upon as a fertile creature and, thus, its foot became a totem for a married couple seeking to populate the world with kids.

That was too easy. Let me do another. How about getting out of bed on the wrong side? Here's what I discovered. It appears you crawl into bed on either the left or right side. When you get up, however, you're supposed to do the opposite. Say you get into bed, sober or slightly sloppy, on the right side. When you rise, stupider than ever, with all your regrets intact, then you should get out of bed on the left side. Vice versa. But here's the catch. In ancient Roman times, when you rose from bed, you were expected to put your right foot down first. For Romans, left—as in left-handed people—was considered "evil." Do you want more? The Romans believed entering a house with the left foot was bad form. That's why a noble family would have a slave—or a household employee dressed in a tunic—watch eagle-eyed how the guest stepped into the house. That employee was a *footman*.

We mostly snicker at ancient superstitions. Gullible us, we follow fake news and influencers who don't look like their photos when you meet them in person. Gone are the superstitions with the strange-sounding phrases like "going whole hog," "to eat one's hat," "once in a blue moon," "to run the gauntlet," "to let the cat out of the bag," "to put a flea in one's ear," and so on. Who believes in the four-leaf clover? Carrying a bride over the threshold? The phrase "not to be sneezed at"? Pointing at a rainbow causing freckles? Or the sad news that your neighbor "kicked the bucket"?

This book has it all, twenty-five chapters, addressing births, the rituals of courtship and marriage, death and mourning, everyday courtesies like shaking hands and saying "God bless you" when a person sneezes, medicine (the staff and serpent as a symbol is explained), parliamentary procedure (Here! Here!), and so many others that speak of our human nature.

Your influencer is nearing the end of this review. Again, I'm not superstitious, but occasionally I will stall, reflect on my stay on the planet, and shiver as if a ghost eerily passed through me. This morning my cat came into the bedroom and meowed. Was there significance in his kitty greeting?

No, it was just a cat exercising his right to free speech.

And last night a fly orbited my cheeseburger. Did it foretell imminent death? No, I shooed the fucker away and ate heartily.

Or last week, when a Tex-Mex poet once again arrived at my front door. We ate, talked stupid in two languages, then ate and drank a lot more. We saw double, then we saw nothing after lowering ourselves to the floor, our shitkickers still on. Hangovers for both of us the next day, then Trader Joe's menudo from a can, the best we could do in a pinch. My mouth was dry, full of chicken feathers. I didn't feel good, but my friend felt worse—the head-band he'd been wearing on his forehead the night before was now around his neck. At the stove, I tossed a flour tortilla on the back burner, watched it puff up with an air pocket, spark at the edges, and blacken slightly, the way I like it. When I flipped it over to toast the other side, the face of Jesus was staring at me. *Ay, Santa María!* I felt my knees buckle, as if genuflecting.

"Look at this," I yelled at the Tex-Mex poet.

"*Que?*" he groaned in return.

"Get your *nalgas* over here!"

He came into the kitchen, shirtless, his tattooed belly a display of several cuss words in Spanish. He was breathing in, breathing out, as if he had just run around the block. The tattooed words expanded, then shrank, on one of the ugliest brown bellies I've ever seen. "Whatta you yellin' 'bout?" he asked. Then he saw.

At the stove, he and I both crossed ourselves in the name of the Father, Son, and Holy Spirit. Even the tribe of empties on the kitchen counter were tinkling with fear at the appearance of Jesus's face on a tortilla.

Now that was an omen if ever there was.

DESIGNING APPAREL
THROUGH THE FLAT PATTERN
By Ernestine Kopp, Vittorina Rolfo, et al.

A COUPLE OF CHILLY NIGHTS AGO I INFORMED MY wife that I would like to go into medicine. She didn't bother to respond. I added that I would eventually work for Doctors Without Borders. Again, no response. I then said that she would be my first patient. She finally sighed and lowered the above-titled reference book, a hefty monster printed on thick paper and coming in at 507 pages.

She allowed herself to smile, but the words that came out of her mouth were not joyful. She declared: "I would rather have a chimpanzee operate on me than you."

This got me smiling. I was invited to proceed with the conversation, even after last night's spat over an end table that I'd spray-painted orange without telling her. I swigged my beer. "Carolyn," I said, "the chimpanzee will be the surgical nurse."

"The surgical nurse?" she asked, in a near whisper.

"You know, the nurse who hands the doctor the scalpel and the cheese grater."

"The cheese grater?" my wife wondered aloud.

I also imagined a chimp handing me a bottle opener followed by a corkscrew, all the while chewing a mouthful of peanuts. I swigged my beer and let the moment enlarge. I saw the chimp again—his nametag read "Ralph"—wiping my sweaty brow with a gym sock.

When the phone rang, Carolyn made her escape, which allowed me to claim the comfy armchair. I picked up the book, a revised fifth edition. It was so large that I needed both hands to hold it. I thumbed a few pages. Like, dang, it did in fact resemble a medical textbook with charts and complicated outlines and a metric conversion table (inches to centimeters) at the end. I grimaced. This reference book is all about sewing from flat patterns; it didn't make any sense to me.

I pondered my wife's pastime, which may have begun when she was a seven-year-old, cutting out paper dolls in the mid-1950s. I was massively confused, yet in awe of my wife. Follower, this may take a while, but here's some of what's described in the book: Seams & Darts on Basic Slopers; Truing Darts for Slopers and Patterns; Hem Allowances; Dart Manipulation; Yokes and Decorative Seams; Elimination of Darts into Back Yokes; Princess Line Front Waist from Two Dart Sloper; Bolero Type Vest with Shawl Collar; Convertible Collar; Two Piece Kimono Sleeve; Raglan Armhole & Waist Variations; Flared Tiered Skirt; Tab Openings for Waists. And I was only on page 30.

I was at a loss for words. My wife is totally smart, I told myself. Now how could I make her happy? That night, I decided to operate on her and remove from her skull the memory of the orange end table. The operating theater? Our bed. I tiptoed downstairs and approached her as she was propped up, all snuggly, reading an Anita Brookner novel, some civilized adventure about a second cup of Earl Grey in fine china. She looked up at me: *What?*

As I approached, she blinked at me, blinked like a little fawn. "You know what," I said.

"No, I don't know what." Blink, blink, blink.

Disrobing, I said, "You need to take off your clothes."

She put her head under the covers, sending the Anita Brookner novel flying to the floor. The fine china must have broken upon landing.

Again, I repeated that she would have to take off her clothes. I explained that the operation would take about fifteen minutes, maybe a little longer if I found something that really needed attention. I picked up the novel and placed it on the lacquered bench next to the bed. I heard her say from under the covers,

"Dr. Sawbones, the anesthesia is working. I'm going to sleep. See, I'm snoring." She produced loud snores that could have cut through fabric.

And I, fresh from the shower, was forced by the Hippocratic Oath to put my sterilized scalpel back in the junk drawer.

THE SHORTEST HISTORY OF ITALY
By Ross King

A TENNIS BUDDY OF MINE PONTIFICATED, CIGAR IN
hand, that the only way to get Covid these days (spring 2025)
was to lick a doorknob. How did he come up with such an ugly
image—a tongue scooping up the virus in one moist swab?
I grimaced at his unofficial medical update. He didn't know beans
about medicine. And he's a hack at tennis.

Now I sigh and pout, suddenly an invalid. Earlier in the week,
in my dotage, I must have licked a doorknob because here I am on
the couch, the virus unrolling like invisible cigar smoke from my
nostrils. It's day three for your influencer: chills, cough, headache,
massive amounts of stupidity to go along with the mucus, with my
eyes—usually bright as dimes—dim as pennies. Yet, followers, I'm
still committed, I'm still with you, and it appears—I look downward at the paperback in my lap—that I'm reading about Italy and
its first days, circa 800 B.C.E., with refugees seeking asylum from
war-torn Greece. Of course, Italy was not called Italy then, but the
refugees, in flimsy boats, would have rowed madly toward shore
even if it had been called Fresno. They wanted to touch land.

The founding of Italy is all about myth. The Greek refugees
risk the Ionian Sea. They arrive on the shore, push the locals
around, colonize the land, establish a quick hierarchy of rulers,
and after a fair time invent their heritage: twins named Romulus
and Remus suckling a she-wolf. Do the twins beam at each other
with brotherly love? No—Romulus kills his brother Remus, for
reasons that are unclear to me. The date of the founding of this
new land? April 21, 753 B.C.E.

After Romulus, hereditary kings ruled, with varying temper-
aments (usually vengeful, bloodthirsty, and lascivious). Then a
new order of kings took office—the patchwork of city-states slowly

melded into what we recognize as Italy, the boot-shaped country. Within 200 years, the kings, now called emperors, see that their cities function with a semblance of law and order. They initiate roads, aqueducts, architecture (the Colosseum!), seafaring trade, agriculture, high art, gladiators, armies, bathhouses, toilets—in other words, these emperors got things done. Meanwhile, there were invaders from all corners, among them the formidable Carthaginians of North Africa. The scariest warrior-leader was Hannibal, whose name itself had the male citizens pissing their togas. I mean, come on, if I'm facing a crazed general on top of an armored elephant, shooting arrows and hurling spears, I'm muttering, in a dialect no longer spoken, "Yikes!" Then I'm taking the first chariot out of town.

Does Crassus mean anything to you? In 55 B.C.E., he was the richest Roman, kind of like Jeff Bezos, but his wealth came from agriculture and the slave trade, possibly outright thievery from the national treasury. He was chummy with government officials and high-ranking military types, such as Caesar and Pompey, both of whom were loved (and feared) by the masses. Together, they were known as the First Triumvirate, the big three. They were godlike, yet human and suspicious of all who came to them daily requesting one thing or another.

They were also ambitious. Crassus intended to show his two compatriots that he was no pushover. He formed an army and marched off to battle the Parthians (think Iraq and Iran). He was killed in battle, with arrows stuck in him like pins in a voodoo doll. His head was severed and used that evening of his death as a prop in a play by Euripides (no joke here—see page 22).

Pompey, jealous of Caesar's exploits, planned to assassinate his rival, who was off fighting against a Germanic tribe. A month passed, then two more, a year almost. Caesar returned triumphantly from the boondocks north of the Alps. The citizens lined the streets to cheer his arrival. With a hero's welcome, he basked in glory. Pompey seethed. He made his move, failed, and quickly got out of town. But Caesar pursued the traitor and, on a beach in Greece, beheaded him. There was no play this time; instead, Pompey's head was kicked into the sea.

All this, readers, sounds implausible, but is as true as Wednesday follows Tuesday. On the evening of Pompey's gruesome death, Cleopatra is smuggled into Caesar's tent. She is hidden in a mattress, which is ceremoniously unrolled onto the carpeted floor. Her charms are put to use that very evening (see page 24). Nine months later, Cleopatra names her son Caesarion, "Little Caesar" (foretelling a restaurant chain?).

Caesar returns to Rome, once again a hero and with a new status—emperor. Of course, not all goes went for Caesar. Though aware of the danger that lurked in the palatial hallways, he was boisterous in his imperial role, let his guard down, and got it one afternoon. His rivals cornered him, swords drawn, and stabbed him multiple times. According to Shakespeare (centuries later), his last words were, "You too, Brutus." Then mortally wounded Caesar staggered like a vaudeville actor and collapsed against a statue of Pompey. Do we have irony here? Not sure.

Was your basic Roman emperor a long-lived figure? Sometimes yes, sometimes no. Here is a list—and a long one—of the assassinated emperors: Gaius (Caligula), Claudius, Galba, Vitellius, Domitian, Commodus, Pertinax, Didius Julianus, Geta, Carcalla, Macrinus, Elagabalus, Alexander Severus, Maximinus Thrax, Pupienus, Balbinus, Gordian III, Gallienus, Aurelian, Tacitus, Florianus, Probus, Carinus, Numerianus, Licinius, Severus II, Constans I, Valentinian II, Eugenius, John the Illicit, Valentinian III, Petronius Maximus, Avitus, Maiorianus, Anthemius, and Nepos.

While the emperors were falling over dead, so were others. Here I speak of invaders and troublemakers that preyed on Italy: Macedonians, Celts, Visigoths, Ostrogoths, Amalungs, Longbeards, Franks, Saracens, Normans, Crips and Bloods (not really, followers, just checking if you're still with me), Lombards, Muslim raiders, etc. In essence, Rome was always frantically defending her boot-shaped territory. Yet, while they were dispensing with the barbarians, Italy also was creating art, sculpture, architecture, gardens, science, mathematics, astronomy, philosophy, law, poetry, music, decorative arts, patrons like de Medici, scientists like Archimedes, Copernicus and Galileo, and outright geniuses like Michelangelo, Raphael, and de Vinci. And Petrarch, a favorite of mine.

Tears fill my eyes and spill onto my cheeks. I couldn't touch the hem of that poet's toga.

And how do the Catholics, Rome and the fathering Popes fit in this history? After all, Rome is the center of Christianity. Christians began to arrive in Rome about sixty years after Jesus's crucifixion. This would include a figure who became St. Paul and another figure who became St. Peter. (The latter saint, beheaded, was buried on the site of gently rolling hills called Mons Vaticanus, site of the Vatican.) Nero was the emperor when, in A.D. 64, a fire swept through Rome and leveled the city. The citizens, many homeless, were totally angry, and Nero, who may or may not have ordered the fire, pointed a finger at the early Christians. This did the trick. Some Christians were sacrificed clothed in bloody fur, to make the vicious dogs go crazy. Others were burned alive in Nero's garden, their lit bodies serving as torches as guests strolled in the evening. King writes that Roman citizens were horrified and, shortly after this repulsive display of inhumanity, the number of Christians grew.

I put *The Shortest History of Italy* aside—enough of history. I'm sick and can't finish this book—or my cup of decaffeinated Earl Grey tea. I frown sourly at this cup—I mean, a brand of tea with "Earl" in its name?

Do you have to wait to be ill to pick up a book like this? It's a large question. To read or not to read, particularly history? I'm a little confused and foggy-minded because I'm forgetting much of what I've read. I cough, I blow my nose, I turn the page of *The Shortest History of Italy.* I can only absorb snippets. I'm thinking of those desperate refugees from warring Greece. Eager for survival, they paddled and rowed for days. After so many days under the sun, they might have become deliriously confused. As the approaching land grew larger and more fruitful in their imaginations, they might have stood up in the rocking boat, hugged each other, waved at the trees on the beach. And, yes, they might have yelled, "Ah, Fresno! We've arrived in Fresno!"

I'm in my comfy armchair. I'm mildly delirious too, and not from the sun or dehydration but from Covid. And I don't ever remember licking a doorknob. This I'm sure about.

FUNDAMENTALS OF
CRIMINAL INVESTIGATION
By Charles E. O'Hara

FOOLISH OF ME TO THINK THAT I COULD HOVER
over my wife, scalpel in my gloved hand, and fix whatever was
wrong with her—she's perfect in body and soul. I went to bed
and slept on my face, my snores sawing into the pillow. The next
morning the cat came to meow at me. I woke and scrubbed saw-
dust from the corners of my eyes. My wife, in turn, surfaced from
hiding underneath the bedsheet, which, if I had operated, might
have been the shroud for her body. I shivered at the image, my
darling on a gurney headed toward the front door. In short,
followers, I made the decision not to go into medicine.

Still, I was not finished on expanding my moral right to be
silly. The next night, on the couch with a St. Pauli Girl, I decided
to bother my wife. I asked, "What do you think of me as an FBI
agent?" I sipped my suds, waited for a response and found none
coming. I tilted my head, just slightly. I became curious about
her reading material. I discovered the title of the book in her
hands: *Everyday Fashions of the Forties as Pictured in Sears Catalogs*
(no joke here). I asked several more times about my ambition to
go into law enforcement. Her response was cold silence. She was
engrossed in the wide collars of the time, the skirt lengths, the pleats,
the early use of rayon and elastic. Then, smart me, I whispered,
"I think I hear a rustle outside. Do you hear it?"

My wife looked up. She blinked like a little fawn.

"Could be thieves." We do live in Berkeley, after all, where in
the morning you can go outside and find your car without its tires.
Berkeley is also the place where poets readily steal from each other.
The ungrateful lot.

She sat up and peered out the window, worried, then relaxed.
The only trouble in the yard was the trouble faced by our cat, the

little gentleman in a topmost branch of the Japanese maple. I leapt like a cat now that I had gotten her attention.

"Carolyn," I whispered.

"What?" She waved a hand in front of her. "You smell beery."

"You think I have the smarts to become an FBI agent?" I also explained that it wasn't just beer but St. Pauli Girl lager. I showed her the buxom lass on the label.

My wife winced at me. "Gary, do you think you have too much time on your hands?"

Was that a positive comment? Did she mean I had more years to roam the planet? I again asked if she thought that maybe I could be a new hire for the FBI, a gamble, seeing that I was seventy-three, a geezer.

She retorted, "I see you more as a security guard, not an FBI agent."

I blinked.

"At the farmer's market," she continued.

Farmer's market!

The next day I cracked open O'Hara's book, first published in 1956. I was going to bone up on whatever the 987 pages offered. I licked a finger, my DNA on the page now, and read the first sentence of Chapter 1: "A criminal investigator is a person who collects facts." The author goes on to say that investigation is an art, not a science. I liked what I read. My confidence rose, like a small red balloon. I'm familiar with art but not hard science, other than that blood circulates in the body; hair grows on heads, in armpits, around private parts, and, if you reach your seventies, out of your nostrils; and air exits our mouths along with words and stupid declarations that can get elected to the highest office.

The author is thorough for his time, the 1950s. Here, followers, are the topics found in the table of contents: the investigator's notebook; photographing the crime scene; inter-

views; interrogations; admissions, confessions, and written statements; informants; missing persons; surveillance; undercover
assignments; burning buildings; automotive fires; homosexuality;
other forms of sexual perversion; pickpockets; confidence games;
loan sharking; truck robbery; forgery; blood and other body
fluids; post-mortem examination; time of death; gunshot wounds;
interviewing witnesses; latent fingerprints; laundry and dry
cleaning marks; physical descriptions; tests for intoxication;
hijacking; hair and fibers; handwriting identifications; typewriting
identification; illegible writing; anonymous letters; inks; modus
operandi; ultraviolet radiation; arrests and apprehensions; searches
of a person; raids. And more.

A lot to ponder, a lot to learn. I gleaned the pages regarding
intoxication. Here's what I discovered: "when the alcohol concentration is greater than 1.5 parts per 1000, the person is under
the influence; at three parts per thousand, he is intoxicated; at
four parts per thousand, he becomes unconscious; after five parts
per thousand, he will probably die." OK, I get it. This is science,
like medicine is a science. But as a poet and influencer, I have
my own definition. For me, intoxication is a Tex-Mex poet on the
front porch throwing up chili verde on your prize-winning azalea
bush, each heave from the shitfaced hombre executed with a
yodel. Intoxication is the poet crawling back into the house and,
feet splayed, getting comfy on the carpeted floor. The last words
from his mouth: "Roman, Roman . . . rosebud, rosebud."

I scratch my dome, scratch my cheek; a grand scheme
percolates in my gray matter. I envision a project. Every poet, plus
essayists who write like poets, could create material that I'll call,
let's see, *Latent Dream Stuff from the Bureau of Big Ideas*. With
such a title, we might deserve grant funding! No, wait a minute,
I just remembered. The president took away our pitiful allotment
of public funds.

Indeed, I'm onto something. We poets and writers could enhance the points explained by the author of *Fundamentals of Criminal Investigation*. I glow, I think, I scratch my dome, cheek, and chin. How do we begin? How do we herd poets and writers into this visionary project? I sip my beer, crush the can, consider the water stains on the ceiling—I still see them as my cat's pawprints.

OK, let's consider "time of death." Got to ask a poet—Gary Gildner, for instance—to write about the time of death of his first college car. "Loan sharking" I assign to Ron McFarland, a fisherman—he'll gladly shove his legs into waders and take a few steps into a wild river. "Investigative notebooks . . ." Ted Kooser could do that. "Inks?" Oh, let's see, how about the fine-press publishers Rick and Rosemary Ardinger? They have only to look at their fingers for their subject matter. I go to my bookshelf, scan the titles until I find what I want: the 2022 issue of *The Limberlost Review*. My eyes explore the names on the cover. I see the literary culprits. I'll call upon Sherman Alexie, Maureen McCoy, Jay Parini, Clay Morgan, Jim Heynen, Jim Dodge, Rachel Teannalach, Ted Kooser, Ed Sanders and that mysterious person called *And More*, who in other magazines also goes by *And Others* . . . They'll play along, wordsmiths all, tinklers with notions from their own bureaus of silly ideas.

A career in medicine or law enforcement—nah.

The days lope along. Monday rushes to Thursday and Thursday jumps right to Sunday dinner. Sunlight on the dining room wall, then shadows creeping up the wall. I artistically toss a salad with two mismatched forks. I juggle the salt and pepper shakers and play peek-a-boo with my napkin I beam at my wife. She provides me with a three-second smile. Then, after heaping lettuce onto her plate, she speaks her mind. "Gary, you think you have too much time on your hands?"

At seventy-three, not enough.

THE STORY OF THE
SHIPWRECKED SAILOR

By Gabriel García Márquez

I FIRST READ THIS SAILOR'S YARN WHEN I COULD
step into the ocean and swim out far enough that my toes couldn't
touch bottom. *Fear?* I asked myself, as I bobbed in the water. I spit
sea water back into the sea—*what fear?*

But, followers, that was thirty-five years ago. The sun disappeared many times on the horizon, the gulls angled away and
returned with more of their kind. Now, I'm not so brave. I could
let the waves roll over my bare feet, maybe darken my pant legs, all
the adventure I allow myself at this age. I'll watch the waves roll
in, and the surfers, lean dark figures on their boards, enjoy themselves in the sparkling sunlight. Just those pleasurable moments
would complete my day.

This short book features a Colombian sailor named Luis
Alejandro Velasco, who in 1955 was washed overboard during
an unexpected storm. One quick-thinking sailor threw a life
raft into the sea after him—good luck, my friend! The story was
presented in fourteen installments in *El Espectador*, a surefire
reading experience for the entire country of Colombia. This
near tragedy embodies bravery, sun blisters, thirst, starvation,
sharks, the addiction of time (our hero was always looking at
his watch), boredom, stargazing, delusional conversations with
a drowned sailor, search-and-rescue planes, fury at his bad luck, all
in ten days on the sea. The full title of this 109-page book?

The Story of a Shipwrecked Sailor
who drifted on a life raft for ten days
without food or water, was proclaimed a national hero
was kissed by beauty queens, was made rich through publicity,
and then spurned by the government
and forgotten for all time

The title says it all: a sailor's struggle for survival. The story is full of terror, yet an entertaining page-turner. We feel for the sailor, chew our fingernails with worry and excitement. During my second time with this book, I sipped my beer while our hero, Luis Alejandro Velasco, drifted on the Caribbean Sea under the blazing sun. He survived the ten days by quenching his thirst with the rare rain shower. Twice he feasted on seagulls that he battered against the hull of his life raft and tore into with gusto. He also maintained his sanity by thinking of the woman he left stateside in Mobile, Alabama. Her name was Mary Address, jokingly called Maria Dirección by his Spanish-speaking chums.

On day ten he washed up on the shore and dragged himself to the shade of a coconut tree. He tried to split open a coconut but failed. He had no strength—and no implement to crush the nut. In time, he was found, carried reverently to a village, provided with a bed and a doctor's appraisal. Eventually his health was restored with generous meals. He even became a legend: tickets were sold to see the survivor. Later still, back in Colombia, he assumed the role of a national celebrity. The president honored him with a medal. He promoted a brand of shoe (of the sort he wore on the life raft) that was too tough to eat. He also promoted chewing gum and raved about the durability of a brand of watch. The moment was his and Luis cashed in.

Darwin is right. All living things, including people, struggle for life and to stay alive however they must. We abhor the thought of not existing. And we're also a curious sort. While revisiting this very short book, I sipped my beer then glugged away, a willing participant of this seafaring adventure. I had to wonder what gull feathers tasted like.

THE JOY OF DRINKING
By Barbara Holland

I HAVE FINALLY DISCOVERED THE ROOTS OF OUR drinking culture. Roughly put, the author of *The Joy of Drinking* explains why our ancestors drank: for the pleasure of socializing and, in turn, escaping personal hardships back in the two-bedroom cave. Yes, even cavemen and cavewomen cried into their suds, possibly to the country-western music of their time.

Our nomadic ancestors had grown tired of going here, going there, living on this, living on that. They settled down to raise crops by doing the slash-and-burn thing. With rudimentary tools, a grasp of seasons, and the magical blessing of rain, they became farmers who grew wheat, barley, rice, potatoes, and fruit trees. They learned to dry plums, figs, apples, and grapes. Eventually they added tomatoes, cucumbers, and easily grown squash that no one has liked since Fred Flintstone.

That's my take on early farming, plus the quickly evolving notion of assembling in tribes—tribes that grew into villages. These previously nomadic people became more friendly to strangers, not their typically vengeful selves toward outsiders. They prospered, grew taller through better nutrition, and became more creative with clothes, shoes, and jewelry. They looked toward the night sky and discovered their spiritual selves. *God*, they thought, *life is totally good.*

Or something like that.

This short book is a history lesson, though readers know that we forget historical facts as quickly as they enter our brains. But let's remember this: there's a job in the world called archaeological chemistry. One such expert is Patrick McGovern, who put it this way: "The domestication of plants, construction of complex villages and production of fermented drinks [developed] at the same time in both regions."

What regions were those? A prehistoric village in southern China and an unspecific oasis in the Middle East. And when did those people first hoist a proper drink to their lips? Ten thousand years ago, just about the time a caveman with a name like Musk-Ug invented the wheel. The archaeological chemist did his research: in both instances a residue of wine was found in clay jugs; this residue consisted of rice, hawthorn fruit, and wild grapes. Ah, our first cocktail—and our first happy hour.

Our forebearers had been drinking before that, of course. Possibly as early as 12,000 B.C., while cutting rough paths through the European forests. There they paused in their tracks, wiped their sweaty brows, looked up and considered the bands of possums climbing trees, eating apples in late autumn, and falling out of the trees, drunk. *Drunk?* Yes, the possums fell from sucking on fermented apples, possibly with silly grins on their sweet little faces. That's a guess and my hope—that the possums were happy when they landed, with a thud. I've known poets who have fallen over drunk; however, none of them was grinning. They were just stinking drunk, these comrades and cousins, MFA graduates who slept on carpeted floors or in the backseats of their cars.

We toasted each other then, and we toasted the heavens. Think of Dionysus and Bacchus, the gods of myth, watching our mayhem from above. Even Jesus turned water into wine to keep the party going; he understood the general populace. The Sumerians made eight kinds of beer—a hearty toast to them—while an Etruscan fresco from 2000 B.C. shows a party scene in which a beautiful woman is holding a bowl for guests to throw up in. And since we're on the subject of turned stomachs, there was a rich Roman merchant, who had, next to his banquet hall, an anteroom used exclusively for heaving your wine and ravioli.

Mark Twain reportedly quipped, "Sometimes too much drink is barely enough." Clever him, clever us. We humans brewed our poison in all parts of the world, except northern Canada.

The Eskimos had no wheat, barley, or rice to stir up batches of the good stuff.

Followers, let me make you thirsty. Here are some choice alcoholic beverages from around the world: yappo from Venezuela, chicha from the Andes, sack from England, cock ale also from England, rum from Jamaica, ouzo from Greece, whiskey from Ireland and Scotland, champagne from France, sambuca from Italy, vodka from Russia, applejack from colonial America, madeira from Portugal, the martini from 1940s Manhattan, sake from Japan, lonkero from Finland, soju from Korea, pisco sour from Peru, and Two-Buck Chuck from Trader Joe's.

This influencer is thirsty, very thirsty. Yet, I continue.

The view on coffee in 1600s England: "base, black, thick, nasty bitter, nauseous puddle water." Pub owners urged the authorities to ban coffee for all men under sixty. This was before Starbucks and the legions of coffee addicts began roaming the streets with cups in hand. (In my mind, coffee is meant for the early hours of a new day—and two cups, max.)

Barbara Holland is an independent writer. This book, like her previous books, doesn't have a single footnote. But I have confidence in her reporting. She writes, "Alcohol is an Arabic word, *Al-kuhul*. It means 'to sweat.'" I believe that. And I believe this: in England the drinking establishments at one time were called pubs, taverns, and tippling houses. For a brief spell, it was a toss-up as to which name was best for the places where locals could get shitfaced. Imagine the yarns, squabbles, gossip, songs, toasts, dancing, games of darts, arm wrestling, outright whoring, and the upheaval of vomiting. The debate was settled around 1700: "pub" won out, though some establishments still called themselves taverns. Tippling houses? The name disappeared along with the Picts.

This influencer, a major figure in several area codes where there are more trucks than cars, ends this review—and quickly.

It's been a good run, these pages of mine, with the occasional typos and such. Now I'm thinking of my six-pack of St. Pauli Girl. My girlfriend is waiting for me and so is my wife, who is in the comfy armchair reupholstered by the Hungarian craftsman (the Hungarian drink of choice is pálinka). I leave you with this: the word *honeymoon* comes from a time when the bride's father would give a month's supply of mead (made with honey) to the newly married couple. If this is true—and Holland tells me so—then I've been on a honeymoon for fifty years.

ENDNOTES

A River Runs Through It

In my effort at guerilla gardening, I manage a street median outside High Street Presbyterian Church in Oakland's Fruitvale District, where a strip of undernourished soil flows and bends up a long, severely littered street. As I am a member of the church, with a mostly aged congregation, I would like the older congregants to admire beauty when they leave service. God knows, in this area of Oakland, we have little beauty but plenty of dispiriting clutter—what's that mattress leaning against a mailbox all about? What *troca* (truck) did that filthy sofa fall from?

I've enjoyed gardens small and large, public and private, new and old, kept and unkempt, native and non-native. My last jaunt was to view gardens within the old city walls of London—Noble Street Gardens, St. Olave's, St. Alphage Gardens, St. Mary Staining, Postman's Park, Christchurch Greyfriars, and the Barbican. Maintained by city workers and volunteers in lime-colored reflective vests, these pocket gardens, stamp-sized in relation to world gardens, benefit citizens, tourists, and civil servants, plus the frantic insect world. In short, they give pleasure. How could we frown at a moist bed of pansies, some red, some yellow, some purple, as they do their best to hold their faces up in the city wind?

I harbor inside me a wish to create a garden where passersby will slow, reflect on my anonymous handiwork, and believe the world a great place. Am I naïve? Litter, I find, still creeps along this Oakland street and French fries are scattered like severed fingers. Condoms, with frightening bubbles locked inside, must be shoveled with a discarded plastic spoon into a plastic bag.

Why not plant daffodils, I asked myself, a common enough decorative flowering plant—though their springtime careers are as short as those of ballerinas. In October 2012, I bought sixty bulbs from American Meadows, generic types with names like King Alfred, Golden Ducat, Dutch Master, Sorbet, and Miniature Cheerfulness—yes, Miniature Cheerfulness, a daffodil that expressed my motive. I kept one sack of bulbs in the garage and another in the fridge as required for a money-back guaranteed success. On a cool November day my buddy David Ruenzel and I dug mole-like holes into dry earth. We scooted bulbs into the holes, sprinkled fertilizer on them, and covered them with a layer of potting soil. We didn't know what we were doing; we just assumed that a buried bulb is a good bulb, provided it is set tip up. We next watered them by hand, as recommended by the catalog, and poked wooden chopsticks into the ground to mark our plantings. And God favored our unselfish Christian effort because in January they began to appear—up King Alfred, I sang, up Golden Ducat and Sorbet, and you, Miniature Cheerfulness, why are you teasing us with your lateness? In spite of the constant litter, the street became instantly beautiful, eye candy for older men like me. But I realized immediately that sixty flowers were hardly any display at all. What was I thinking? The median needed the colorful madness of more—lots more!

The next year, for an annual fee of ten dollars, I joined the Northern California Daffodil Society, proof that I'm entering another stage of life. The first meeting was at the Alden Lane Nursery in Livermore, and the members were debating a small point in their mission statement when I arrived. The debate was serious because none of the members greeted me. True, their eyes lifted to acknowledge my quiet presence, but no hearty hello followed. Engaged with the issue on the floor, they were single-minded in arriving at consensus. Thus, I sat in a folding chair with my hands on my lap and did my best to suppress a yawn—the discussion reminded me of a heady English faculty meeting. After the matter was settled, the members stood up, stretched, and then locked their eyes on me. I was greeted by smiles and proffered hands.

I helped myself to coffee in a Styrofoam cup and, after a few minutes of mingling, returned to my folding chair. It was then the auction followed. I was given a paddle to hold up if I wished to bid on heirloom daffodil bulbs. *Costly little babes*, I thought. When the auction was done, however, I came away with Polly's Pearls, Goddess Chispas, Earlicher, Bravoure, Golden Dawn, Fragrant Rose, Storyteller—bulbs that meant nothing to an amateur like me but indicated to the members my willingness to open my wallet. I was ready to join their enchanted lunacy! What was twenty dollars to me? Forty dollars? Sixty dollars? (These specialty bulbs were devalued when I returned home. I told my wife that I got them for a dollar each, as I didn't want to give her permission to go wild with jewelry purchases.)

The bulbs would go into my personal garden and prove to be colorful showstoppers, friendly depots for bees, and, yes, prize-winners in February's show. Once a radical Chicano poet with shoulder-length hair, now I would earn six ribbons for my daffodils, including one for Best in Show for Small Grower. The ribbons would be kept in my desk drawer, out of the sunlight for I wouldn't want them to fade. I might want to have them framed someday.

But that success was months away. After the meeting in Livermore, I scanned the Internet for affordable varieties from American Meadows, fifty-per-bag assortments. For the street median, it didn't matter if the bulbs were a princely sort, with pedigrees. I was interested in a massive display that would shock neighbors and bystanders and give hope to Presbyterians. That late fall, on my own, I dug in the median nearly two hundred small holes. My gopher-like ambition grew as I clawed at the resistant earth. My fingernails became dark moons of grit, my neck sunburned, my eyelashes covered in dust. Dime-sized sweat dropped from my face into the dry dirt. With a shovel, I cut short the lives of bitter weeds, warning them not to come back. Next time around I would be armed with Roundup.

One day a Mini Cooper pulled up to the median and honked. A young woman, head craned out the window, yelled, "Hey."

Having responded many times to "Hey," I walked slowly to the car with a trowel in my hand. Bending over with my hands on my knees, I saw a young woman with a very short dress, bare legs, and white panties comparable to the daffodil called Ice Follies, $13.95 for a bag of eight. I caught myself assessing her Ice Follies, but swiveled my eyes back to her face, mouth red as Flanders poppies, eyelids blue as hyacinth.

"How can I help you?" I asked

"We be looking for a cannabis club," she said. "Some place close."

Two cars passed, honking, the drivers maddened at the back end of the Mini Cooper, which was jutting out into the street.

"What?" I responded, "What's that?" I winced in confusion, thinking, *Jesus, maybe I need a hearing aid—my wife says I do.*

"We lost," she began again as another car swerved around us.

That's when her friend, a girl as tall as a giraffe in that squat car, leaned over and hollered, "Daddy, the cannabis club! Suppose to be off Thirty-fifth." Her dress was very short too, but her panties were pinkish, like the dazzling beauty called Pink Charm, $6.98 for a bag of eight.

"A cannabis club!" I said, disappointed that the women in the car were not actually lost and I, a citizen volunteering for the betterment of Oakland, was not about to help hook them up with a bag of righteous medical marijuana. After all, these youthful babes were the pictures of health.

"Oh, I don't know about that," I answered, standing straight up and backing away. My trowel, I realized, was bright as a chrome handgun. At that point I should have scratched my old man scalp, maybe even smacked my lips to suggest that my dentures were at home smiling in a jam jar.

The Mini Cooper pulled away, the sassy women laughing. As I returned to work, the sky was dark and heavy, promising rain. The newly planted daffodils could use a natural shower, I thought, an autumnal blessing.

It stormed that evening and all the next day, rain tapping on my roof, rain tapping roofs all over Oakland. Four months later, at the beginning of February, my daffodils began to emerge, the flirty Pink Charms and Ice Follies the first to swagger in the cool spring air. From the right distance, even the ever-present litter resembled flowers.

You Wear It Well

This is me several years ago at the British-themed Jack Wills shop on King's Road in London. With sudden rain, umbrellas were thrust skyward, some like large bright petals and others black as funerals. Hurrying pedestrians knocked into each other. Rain drenched the public, even the stylish dogs in yellow slickers, and leaves choked gutters.

We stepped into this clothing shop, where I shook my shoulders of wetness, while my wife pulled away to inspect the baggy pants bright as toucans that she had spied across the room. I was left to stand in the middle of the store, at a loss for what to do with myself. I then did what my wife was doing—and looked around. I considered the displays mildly amusing. Every item seemed youngish, and the sales help were all young and bright as Christmas candy. The music from the speakers was all electronic garble, the throbbing sounds that robots might dance to.

I found an old velvet chair, got comfy and opened the program of Richard Bean's play *English People Very Nice*, which we had seen in a matinee at the National Theatre. It had been a memorable experience. The play is about Indian immigration to Great Britain and the racist comments uttered by the characters sometimes made me grip the arms of my chair. Overall, I thought the show hilarious and so touching that I expect to see it again. In the program, there was a cartoonish display of great moments in immigration, including a 1904 scene in which worshippers at an ultra-Orthodox synagogue (once a Huguenot Protestant church and later, after the synagogue years, a mosque) were pelted with bacon sandwiches by Jewish anarchists on Yom Kippur. I was imagining this moment of flying club sandwiches when my wife called, "Gary, come here."

I stood up and looked about, ostrich-like, for my wife Carolyn, who is short and can often disappear among the racks of clothes. When she called again, I got moving and found her on the stairwell, waving for me to hurry over. I followed with a hand on the rail for balance, eyeing my every step. Soon I was standing before a wall and asking, "What am I looking at?"

"The jacket," she remarked, pointing.

Since there was a display of six jackets, I risked, "Which one?"

"The maroon one—get it down and try it on."

The maroon jacket was made of heavy wool and displayed a school crest. I had to stand on tiptoe to reach it. The lining was yellowish from age. I put it on and shrugged at the cuffs.

"Look in the mirror," my wife commanded.

I turned and saw myself, shoes splayed, jeans wrinkled, thinning bangs wild from wind and rain. The schoolboy's jacket was stylishly hip. I turned sideways and recognized that, in my jeans, my butt didn't look as if it had fallen that far. *You could pull this off*, I told myself. I inhaled so that my paunch disappeared, a temporary liposuction that lasted no more than seconds.

I stripped the vintage jacket off and handed it to my wife, who began to search for a price tag. Finding none, she walked upstairs with me in tow. She called to a young man in periwinkle-colored trousers, "How much is this?"

The young man wore bright red sunglasses on top of his head. He approached in leather boaters, wearing no socks; the cuffs of his trousers ended around the tops of his ankles. He took the jacket and hunted for a price tag, his face crumpling. The hunt ended when the clerk behind the counter hollered, "Scott, it's not for sale. It's display."

The clerk's voice was high, as if on tiptoes. He was very young and wore a boyish part in his hair. Nevertheless, he appeared to be the boss of the moment, the one who directed the even more youthful staff to go here, go there. He sent the boy in the boaters back to his station on the second floor.

"Not for sale?" my wife asked. She seemed bewildered at this piece of news. Like, what was the world coming to if you couldn't buy what was hanging on the wall at a store!

"It's for display, ma'am," the clerk explained. He was wearing orange pedal pushers and a striped T-shirt that hugged his lean body. Unlike many of his generation, his throat was not inked with an undecipherable tattoo.

"Why?" my wife demanded.

He said that the jacket was for display, then remarked, in a prideful confession, that the shop had previously sold an identical jacket—to Rod Stewart. He had let something out of the bag, and my wife glared.

"Then why don't you sell this one to us?" my wife asked, with a little flint in her voice. She had taken possession of the jacket.

The young man stalled. "Because," he replied, blinking a set of pretty eyes at my wife. "Because, oh, how do I say this . . ."

What he said was that they had sold the same maroon school-boy jacket to Rod Stewart because Rod was a cherished celebrity, hinting that I was just a man off the street, a husband and nothing more. He looked out onto the street, his attention captured by the toot of a taxi.

My wife jumped in. "But do you know who my husband is?"

His eyes slowly moved from my wife to me. He pondered me for a second and answered, "No, but I think you're from New York—am I right?"

"He's a famous writer. In America, everyone knows him." She added that we were from California but didn't say our second home was in Fresno.

I felt embarrassed, but also enlightened at the power of the human will. For the first time in our thirty-eight years of marriage, I viewed Carolyn as a true, go-for-broke shopper. But really! A "famous writer" is a dead person who has his or her sober image on a coffee cup. And hadn't two of my last books been remaindered, with others, like lemmings, ready to follow them over the cliff?

The clerk gazed at me with eyes clear as unpolluted sky, so young this boy was. After a moment, he said, "I like novels if I can see the movie first."

He pondered me for a few hard seconds. *Maybe he is a writer of note,* the lad was thinking, or perhaps he just resembles my gramps. Finally, he confided, "You know, sir, you have the same build as Mr. Stewart."

Rod and me? Remarkable.

"Let me check something. What is your name, sir?"

"Gary Soto," my wife answered. "Kids love his books."

The young clerk turned away, walking briskly to the counter. When he opened a laptop computer, his face, already bright, brightened even more with reflected light. His fingers began to scramble across the keys.

Meanwhile, my wife and I cut across several islands of long-sleeve jerseys with British overtones, then passed a table of impossibly slim-fitting jeans, stopping finally at a cubbyhole display of jackets. While I rummaged absently, an obvious novice, she speedily peeled away one jacket after another. She was now frantic in her quest to make me appear dapper (I was in my late fifties at the time) and mildly upset that my credentials as a writer were suspect. It didn't matter that she had described me to the clerk as a bestselling author, not a poet with a couple of lucky textbook hits that made a nice seasonable income. But even if I was not Rod Stewart rich, he and I shared the same build. Wasn't that worth something?

"I hope we get it," she muttered as she stood at the rack of jackets, yanking at the sleeves, searching for one that said *Gary*.

I spent my time ogling the price tags. The jackets were all wool, all 1960s retro, all damn expensive. I was pondering a tag marked down from 150 pounds to 85 pounds in vicious red when my wife said, "This is nice."

I tried on the jacket. It fit, and I figured it would fit Mr. Stewart too. We were of the same build and of the same era, though he was slightly older, of course. Despite his age, he was trying to regroup and discover new music. I had hair like his once, when I was in my mid-twenties. In those days, I had sported his trademark rooster look. But in that department Rod was the clear winner: his hair, though tinted, remained bushy, while mine went with the wind.

The clerk returned and said cheerfully, "I looked you up." He halted in front of Carolyn but spoke of me. "He *is* famous. We can sell the jacket, I think." The young man explained that he had to talk to the regional manager, who was not present, then left, flipping open his cellphone.

My wife veered off to the sweaters and began ripping through them, while I used the wait time to pick up a couple of pairs of argyle socks. They were priced at ten pounds a pair—no wonder the staff didn't wear socks.

When the clerk returned within minutes, he informed us that, yes, the jacket could be sold. He and Carolyn haggled over the price while I drifted away to look at the sweaters I would not buy.

In the end, we bought the schoolboy jacket with the crest and bronze buttons as well as another jacket my wife had located. We left Jack Wills, my wife a few steps in front of me, an invincible force when she sets her mind to shopping. We looked around, squinting because the sun had come out. The sky was blue as that young clerk's eyes. It was humid, time for my mouth to pucker up to a proper drink. But Carolyn had stopped when she spied a women's shoe store with a half-off sale banner across the street.

"Aren't you exhausted?" I asked.

"Exhausted? Yeah, but so?"

She told me to hurry up—the light was about to turn red.

I, a husband and nothing more, followed just behind her.

The Fab Three

I read in the local newspaper that a Beatles tribute band would play a free concert at Orinda Theatre Square. *Why not*, I thought. My wife loved—still loves—their music. After all, the quartet's catchy, jingle-like melodies were part of our youth. But how would we dress? My wife's peasant dresses and mod-squad skirts no longer hung in the closet, while my bellbottoms and Nehru shirts were long gone. In the end, we opted for swank, but not real swank— jeans and a blazer for me, with loafers and groovy argyle socks, and an empire dress with sandals for Carolyn. We figured that we had to play it up. My wife even debated whether to go braless.

Early in the evening we drove to Orinda, parked the car, and found the tribute band. They were set up behind the Orinda Theatre in a corridor of restaurants that was nearly empty on a Wednesday evening. There was no crowd to speak of, only a single pigeon eyeing the threesome.

Threesome?

"Oh," my wife cried quietly. I could read her mind: John must be the missing one, John assassinated thirty-plus years ago, before the foursome could settle their bickering, regroup, and write more jingly tunes. If not for his murder, the whole world would have stopped fighting and listened. Bellbottom pants would never have gone out of style!

The tribute Beatles were in their sixties, white-haired and chubby, and carelessly dressed. Ringo was short and chubby; Paul was short and sort of chubby; George was tall and chubby enough to rest his guitar on the globe of his belly. Still, for the moment, they were the Beatles—or most of the Beatles.

When my wife waved, George smiled. He was young enough to have his original teeth. His hair, though, was thin and revealed a lobster-pink scalp. He was not clad in Sgt. Pepper attire but in a bulky windbreaker with the emblem of a fishing club. His socks were white!

The band, hired by the City of Orinda to liven up the plaza, had already been playing but not, apparently, to screaming fans. The outlook for that possibility brightened upon our arrival and increased further when minutes later two women appeared. Sadly, the women had neglected to dress in hippie getups; they were attired in polyester pantsuits and carried large plastic shopping bags. One pointed to the bench next to ours. With a newspaper, she whisked the seat of leaves and invisible dust before settling, hen-like, on the bench.

The band began "Michelle," a song considered Frenchy in our day. The bass player who sang lead did not resemble Paul McCartney; he looked more like our insurance agent. Ringo tapped a simple beat and George played rhythm guitar. As Paul thumbed the bass, the three-chord melody touched me, touched us—even touched the pigeon, who began goose-stepping in a circle. Carolyn scooted closer to me. *This is going to be nice*, I purred, *an evening to remember.* We were among an audience of four, not counting the pigeon, at a Beatles tribute concert. When would this happen again?

The song ended with a Beatles-esque bow. Carolyn and I clapped and beamed. I couldn't help but notice, however, that the two women—rude sourpusses—had talked during the song. True, they occasionally stopped their gabbing to look up at the band, but neither showed joy. Their faces were like clouds struggling over a hill, dark and ominous. I surmised they had probably lost the love of good men—*yes*, I told myself, that must be it. The men in their lives had gone away.

Carolyn and I cuddled, both of us deliriously happy. We were a couple, and this was the music of our generation when love was mostly free, just like this concert.

When the band played "Twist and Shout," we figured out that the guitarist was not George but John. The song was John's signature piece, with raw vocals and teenage angst. My own head bobbed, and our knees jerked to the beat. I turned to my wife and smiled as I spied her breasts. My girl *had* decided to go braless—naughty thing.

During this raucous anthem, the manager of the Orinda Theatre appeared. After the song ended with a gusty twang, she approached the band with husky steps; her body language meant business. She complained, not quietly, that the music was too loud and upsetting her patrons in the theater. She instructed the band to please lower the volume.

The band members looked at each other with the sadness of henpecked men. John stepped over cables to the amplifiers and played with the knobs. After the manager left, the band started giggling among themselves. I was afraid that they might unplug their guitars, disassemble the drum kit, and go home. But they were troupers. Their next number was "Help," which John sang, ironically, in a near whisper.

Carolyn and I laughed. We sang what lyrics we could remember, louder than the band. When the song ended, we applauded quietly, as we didn't want that theater manager to return. Then I thought: if she does return, maybe she could bring a bag of popcorn for the pigeon.

They played "I Want to Hold Your Hand," a cue for me to hold Carolyn's hand, and "Drive My Car" in succession. I raised my hands and wrapped them around an imaginary steering wheel, twisting it wildly. I could be silly. After all, there was no one around—or hardly anyone.

Carolyn called out, "How 'bout 'Norwegian Wood'?"

Paul and John blinked at each other, then Paul said, "We only do early Beatles." He hesitated before explaining with a chuckle, "We're not that good."

"Nah!" we—the fan base—sang in harmony.

"You're good," I corrected.

"You're *real* good," Carolyn agreed.

Ringo did a drum roll, and Paul thumbed his bass. They appreciated our eagerness.

"What's your name?" Paul asked Carolyn.

Carolyn told him, and Paul dedicated the next song, "I Saw Her Standing There," to her (the lyrics begin with, "She was just seventeen"). Paul said, "This one goes out to," and took a swig of bottled water, then capped the bottle; he had already forgotten her name.

Carolyn supplied it.

"Carolyn—that's right."

The band started full force, then remembered their directive—shush or else! They played the song softly while we hand-clapped along. When it was over, we applauded softly—this was too much fun.

"Where's George?" Carolyn asked, figuring that, with so few of us, we could talk to the performers between songs.

"He had to work," John answered.

George is moonlighting?

John strummed his guitar, ready to kick-start another song. But he stopped when the women next to us rose to leave, one of them noisily twisting the top of her plastic shopping bag. They had been rudely yakking about some domestic triviality regarding windowpanes throughout the set. Who cared about the gardener who left his gas can on the side of her house? Couldn't they sense this moment would never happen again? Still, I was troubled by their imminent departure.

"If you two leave," I said jokingly, "then there will be only half the audience." The pigeon had already winged itself away.

One of the women squinted, a fissure of lines darkening her brow. "It's not my responsibility to be the audience," she said curtly.

If I had a toupee on my scalp, it would have flown off upon hearing that remark. I did not like this woman. As she and her friend walked away, I was glad their polyester pantsuits didn't fit!

But there was music in the air from the Fab Three!

"This goes out to Carol," announced Sir Paul.

Close enough.

The band played "She Loves You," this time a little louder. When the song ended, John said, "And this next one goes out to Carol."

Carolyn smiled and felt special. They did "A Hard Day's Night" followed up with a reprise of "Michelle," also for Carol, their dedicated groupie, who applauded slightly beyond the permitted sound level. During the eagerness of her clapping, I saw that the naughty girls were pitching left and right.

The Beatles got loud with "Rain," which dispelled their own assessment that they were not good musicians. The song, a favorite

194

of mine, was hauntingly complex, even with only one guitar. John's vocals measured up—who cared if his socks were white?

"Where you folks from?" Paul asked.

"Berkeley," we answered.

"Do you have a business card?" Carolyn asked.

They shook their heads no, all three of them. They asked how we had heard about the concert, and we told them the newspaper.

They did "And I Love Her," sung by Ringo, and "P.S. I Love You," sung by both John and Paul, with harmonies added by Gary and Carolyn, their backup singers. The summer evening was silly, free, and memorable.

Carolyn and I snuggled against each other. We stayed until the very end because, as long as the music played, the Beatles lived on.

Are Your Affairs in Order?

My wife and I are into Season 3 of *Victoria*, the Masterpiece Theatre series that seems as long as the queen's monarchical reign. It's a slow-moving narrative in which a teacup is picked up, put down. Then, for dramatic tension, the camera pans to a terrier that, on cue, lifts a hind leg to squirt on the carpet—a barbarous display in the palace household. It's a series that may continue without me, as I may succumb to boredom, the white flag of defeat raised on my chest. My last words: "The DVD is from the library—don't forget to return it."

But in one episode I was stirred awake when Queen Victoria's ex-prime minister—what's his name again?—appears ill in speech and in ash-colored makeup. He won't last long, I understand—the cough, the squeak of violins behind the cough, his fish-pouting mouth, the poor posture in the velvet chair, along with the makeup, of course. A somber doctor stands before the former PM and declares, "Sir, you should put your affairs in order."

That line of advice perked me up. I, ever forward-thinking, have a living trust, a document that contains more boilerplate than inventive clauses intended to confuse the taxman. Still, it's done, filed away, and what our daughter will search for when my wife and I are no longer on this planet. We will make it easy for her. We'll leave a trail of Post-Its on the hallway wall, which will lead her to my modest office, where a table lamp throws out a yellow glow and a faint Erik Satie sonata plays on my second-hand Bose radio. The final Post-It will say, "The living trust is here, darling."

Our money in the bank and the mutual funds—or a third of that at least—goes to nonprofits, but the house and items inside the house—the possessions from fifty years of marriage—goes to our daughter. She will be forced to declutter: out with the fourteen pairs of reading glasses, out with the dead batteries, the cotton balls and medicines, the everyday cutlery, the tennis rackets, the potted plants gasping for water on windowsills, the shoes moored like boats in our three closets. The boxed food in the pantry? To the Rescue Mission. The books that stand shoulder to shoulder at the front entrance? Perhaps she will divvy them up to those Little Free Libraries that stand in front of houses in Berkeley—some for you, she might sing, some for you, and you, and you. My attempt at playing filmmaker was short lived—one half-hour production titled *The Pool Party*, on VHS cassette. I have plans for its destruction. I'll run over it many times with my huge American car before I go.

But our art collection is worth pondering for its financial worth. Like housing prices, art has gone skyward. This causes worry. Have I hung them in a way that will cause fading from sunlight? Have they been nibbled by insects with a taste for finer things? I ponder, I muse, and I do sums on my fingers. This DeLoss McGraw, purchased in 2014, what would it fetch? This Rupert Garcia bought in 1984? The Carmen Lomas Garza? The Leo Limon? I'm sure that the works of these artists have gone up in value. A month ago, I visited their websites and saw that they are honored and sought after, written about by scholars at universities that don't need street addresses to get their mail.

The artwork, like the Japanese antiques and Mexican folk art, I value for the pleasure they provide. I see them as counterpoints to my poetry. I mean artists and poets should go side by side, right? I'll buy your artwork if you, bearded portraitist with one ear, will drop twenty dollars to purchase a book of mine.

What do I exactly possess? Several pieces by our favorite artist, DeLoss McGraw. From my couch in the living room, I can see an irregularly sized pastel on thick paper, 7 inches by 5 feet, titled *Alice in Wonderland*. Alice is blond, fleet of foot, in a red jumper. There is plenty to see, other figures—and mystical things—of equal metaphorical weight. There's a dove carrying a three-year-old in a hamper-like black cloth; a boy, also blond, briskly walking; a red rocking horse; and yellow starbursts. The background is bluish, with banner colors of red and yellow, and black-and-white stripes that remind me of piano keys. Purchase price in 2014: $3000. Today's value? Let's add another zero, say $30,000, excluding two-day shipping.

Beyond *Alice in Wonderland*, in our tiny, seldom-used dining room, are two sepia-colored paintings by McGraw. Each of these untitled and book-sized works beckons to be viewed. One shows a boy upside down, topsy-turvy, mouth open, surprised by his circumstance. He is flanked by a tall building that reminds me of the Leaning Tower of Pisa—plus a chair and a world that appears hoisted up by the powerful winds of a tornado. There is a balloon in the middle that says: "What is after the universe?"

On the other side of the French doors is its twin. While this one is mostly sepia-colored, here we have a spot of color; this boy is also upside down but wears a blue shirt. The top of the building is roofed in blue and what might be a moon—not a splotch—is also blue. The balloon in the middle says: "What was the right answer?"

The twin portraits were bought in 2006 for $425 each. I drum my fingers on my thighs, calculating a new price. In less than a minute, I come up with a figure. Value: $36,000 for the pair. That sounds about right.

Without pushing myself off the couch, I can appreciate more of our art collection. If I swivel my head to the right I look upon two more fanciful McGraws, one of which is an artist proof, number 4. It features a boy, about age ten, dressed in a brown suit with fat, grayish rings around his thighs and knees. On his head a bluish cap, with red stripes and, as a bill to the cap, what looks like a canary. There are green, blue, red, and brown animal-like faces that could be masks; then again, they could be faces of quasi-humans who hanker to make the leap into the animal world. Purchase price in 2004: a gift from the artist! I munch on my lower lip and think. A few seconds and my estimate is tabulated. Value: $47,000. Who could argue?

And to the right of this untitled McGraw is yet another untitled McGraw done with pastels on thick paper. It features a young man who is two-thirds slender legs, a human giraffe if there ever was one. His pants are brown, his shirt red, and his cap of hair a light shade of brown. A few inches from his face he holds a stick with an animal mask—the face of a pony or the face of a bear? He's peering through the mask at a bent-back man who grips a lumpish sack. Behind the man there is a red ladder—McGraw loves ladders—and near the top is a fractured house—McGraw loves houses even more. Purchase price in 2003: another gift from the artist. Without much pondering, my internal auction gavel comes down. Value: $145,000. To wit—poets and artists require three meals a day! And we also require our portion of wines produced in French regions that we'll never visit. (Most of us fear flying unless it's by way of dreams.)

Now I must get up from the couch and take myself down the hallway where hang two other DeLoss McGraw pastels. One features the most adorable couple on the face of the planet: my wife and me in our youth, in our beauty, in the spring of our lives. I am holding a house on fire, presumably lit by the bolt of yellow lightning just above our heads and presumably the sensual fire that we would create in our partnership. There are also a red rocking horse, a secondary house, a television on fire, a man-in-the-moon face, a purple and yellow planet, and a whimsy of pinwheels—in short, a Magical Mystery Tour. The work is almost life-size if my wife were to stand next to it. Purchase price in 2003: another gift! Current value: $229,000. Unfortunately for art dealers in New York and in Houston, this piece is not for sale.

Also, in the hallway hangs a hand cut from thick paper and brightly painted—reds, yellows, blues and greens, primary colors that remind us of our first pack of crayons. The title: *Hand*. This image, roughly six times the size of an adult hand, has a map of lines on the palm. The fingers are numbered 1 through 4, and the thumb is numbered 5. What would a palm reader discover? She might read the lines as a lunatic's travails. She might need to bring out her tarot cards or blow the dust off her crystal ball. Purchase price in 2006: yet another gift. Current price: a nonnegotiable $634,000. A steal for the hedge-fund manager with untraceable inside knowledge of the financial markets.

In my office hangs, in semi-dark, another DeLoss McGraw, also untitled, which features gouache images of a red triangle shaped box, a purple ladder, an upside-down chair, a pair of two-tone shoes, a pair of arms, a cart with red-spoked wheels, and a poet leaning forward as if he were flying or falling. How do I know it's a poet? Below the image is my poem "Moving Away," a tender call to my older brother, Rick, to remember our lean years. I view this work daily; no, hourly; no, every ten or twenty minutes when I'm called to my office by the landline—telemarketers are relentless and often begin their prerecorded pitch with, "Hello, seniors!" Here, in this 2-foot-by-3-foot master work, we have further evidence that artists and poets go together. Purchase price in 1998: a gift. Current price: $725,300. Buyer—corporation or upstart techie in jeans and T-shirt—think of it as an investment, and as dues paid to the creative world.

When I do a soldierly about-face, my eyes brighten on another framed gift from overly generous McGraw, Christmas 2016. It's a watercolor sketch inspired by William Shakespeare *and* me—yes, Shakespeare and me. Several years ago, I took a line from the Bard and built my own poem upon that line. Before the creative impulse ended, I had over a hundred poems, all of which began with famous lines, such as "All that glitters is not gold," "Shall I compare thee to a summer's day?" and "We are stuff . . . rounded by sleep." The book of poems, *You Kiss by th' Book*, is still available. I have lots of copies in the garage; Chronicle Books, the publisher, has even more copies in its much larger garage.

Most of the poems in *You Kiss by th' Book* are long, robust, bawdy, wise as Solomon, and teasingly romantic. DeLoss and I had plans to create an art book based on the poems from this collection. This proverb-length one, starting from Othello 1.1.63, caught his eye.

> I will wear my heart upon my sleeve
> And up this sleeve is a trick or two.

And what did my collaborator render on the page? A long, flowing sleeve done in yellow, with a red heart at the center, a white rabbit, and a pair of playing cards—the two of spades and the three of hearts. An errant blue drop is outside the subject. I appreciate the gift, but I may part with it if times get hard. Current price in Ireland: 132,000 euros. In the United States: $147,000. Insured shipping is available. Note: this artwork was done on typing paper and, therefore, has bubbled in places.

I sigh as I come to the end of our horde of McGraws. I'm as ashen as that prime minister in *Victoria*.

It's all over, I think, my artful excursion. Then I remember the file next to the living trust, the one called "DeLoss." It contains ephemeral items such as postcards (with drawings) letters, a single strand of hair, catalogues, an essay written by me, and, in my quivering hands, two rare originals: gouache paintings on watercolor paper. In one, a boy beams his large moon-like face at the viewer; in the other, a boy in a striped shirt looks out the window while the moon with eyes and ruddy cheeks looks in. I admonish myself—why didn't I frame them earlier!

We have other art displayed on our walls. We also have antique Japanese tansus, rare books, one-of-a-kind prints, fine jewelry, and a wedding kimono purchased for my wife on our twenty-fifth wedding anniversary. For insurance purposes I should tally our valuables, lick the lead of a pencil and enter the value of each piece in a book that will be opened by our daughter upon our passing.

And my ghastly film on VHS cassette? After I crush it under the tires of my Chevy Malibu—light bulb here!—I'll send the shards to DeLoss McGraw. Although our collaboration on the Shakespeare project didn't pan out, maybe the sparks of a new idea will color his thoughts. He will pour the contents of my package onto his worktable and study them like a forensic specialist combing through debris. Under his breath, he'll wonder, "Now what do we have here?"

Poet-friendly McGraw could do something with the shards. Perhaps he could create ladders, houses, rocking horses, another Alice, another couple not unlike my wife and me, and moons— lots of moons—from those pieces of a crushed VHS cassette. I am certain that he would send me a shard creation, though I would insist that he permit me to pony up, for he has been so generous in the past! In a letter dated Friday, February 6, he writes, "I really mean this—don't buy my art. Save your hard-earned money. I will trade you. The trade could be more for the both us—if we make a show." He knows that the imaginations of poets and artists are a naturally crazy fit.

As for *Victoria*, the series may go on for several more seasons. An audience exists for this slow-moving history. The queen reigns, lives with (and without) Prince Albert, and obliviously walks in splendor beneath some of the finest artworks in her country. I realize that the art displayed in the series should be of its time or earlier. But think—just think—of a camera panning a palatial ballroom past a Constable and a Turner to a wall of out-of-era DeLoss McGraw paintings! This would stop the wine-sipping audiences on both sides of the Atlantic.

Now we're talking value! *Mucho dinero.* I could shred my living trust and—like a prince—live comfortably ever after.

Some Words about Proverbs

I've played my part as tourist in the Netherlands. In Amsterdam, I skipped out of the way of ring-chiming bicycles. I hoisted mugs of Amstel beer under an awning while an afternoon rain dotted the surface of the Singel canal. I petted the head of an approachable white swan, and I walked through a convention of pigeons, each with a warble of complaint. I poked my head into a bar where marijuana-concocted drinks were drawn noiselessly through plastic straws—the faces of these patrons seemed slow. In Delft, among sightseers loud as geese, I rode a boat down a canal, and, in Enkhuizen, I ate herring while pondering the sea, flat and silvery, under similar clouds that propelled the Dutch ships of 1700. For laughs, I tried on wooden clogs in Utrecht. In Rotterdam, I picked up, then put down, a smutty magazine. I visited The Hague and, little old man that I am, stood before the art that hangs at the Rijksmuseum. At the Keukenhof garden, I lowered my nose into a tulip, then walked along beds of tulips, judging them as nothing but outrageously colorful show-offs. Big deal that they are so glorious!

I'm familiar with the Netherlands. Along with whatever else I learned by towing a roller bag over bridges and down narrow pathways, the faint smell of urine rising from graffiti-marked walls. I'm also just educated enough to recognize the works of Pieter Bruegel the Elder (as well as the Younger), but I was unfamiliar with his allegorical painting *Netherlandish Proverbs*. That painting graced a card I received from Professor Wolfgang Mieder, eminent folklorist, who kindly informed me that he had written a blurb for my forthcoming book, *Meatballs for the People: Proverbs to Chew On*. Smiling, I read Wolfgang's note, then turned the card over to size up Bruegel's painting, completed in 1559. What struck me immediately was the busy nature of the townspeople depicted, all of whom seemed to be on the lunatic fringe—or, perhaps, they were the starring cast in an experimental film! On first glance, I registered neither the title of the artwork nor the fact that it was from Professor Mieder. I let my eyes rove over the colorful scene, slow on the uptake, unaware that behind each contorted citizen or set of citizens, was a Dutch proverb. What I saw was a frightening madness packed with detail. My private thought? *God, I'm glad I don't live there.*

Then I did some Internet research and graduated to a higher understanding. Now I see both the artistic light and the historical light. Why hadn't I been awake to the painting's meanings? After all, the card itself provides scholars with the word proverb in numerous languages. Full disclosure: I did not lower my face to one of those straws sunk in a marijuana milkshake.

What did I learn? That in Pieter Bruegel the Elder's master-piece, there are arguably 115 depictions of proverbs. In 1903, a scholar by the name of Louis Maeterlinck identified 32; in 1915 Johannes Bolte identified 69; in 1923 Wilhelm Fraenger noted

92; then, in 1957, in a monograph meant only for specialists, Jan Grauls reduced this figure to 85. But in 1973, scholar R. Grosshans raised the ante to 118. And in 2016, I gazed not upon pictorial proverbs but a topsy-turvy scene of village life. My thoughts were so subdued by the technical brilliance of the painting that I didn't figure allegory was at play.

So, is *Netherlandish Proverbs* merely a game for scholars, a high-level version of *Where's Waldo?* When we look at this wonderfully rendered and iconographic masterpiece, should our goal be to find select proverbs rather than an overall meaning? "Here's a proverb," an alert viewer might say. "Here's another one, and yet another." The search would involve intelligent gamesmanship, maybe wrong guesses, maybe just academic nonsense. Still, it would be amusing—and good for the noodles upstairs.

I also learned this bit of trivia: that the son, Pieter Bruegel the Younger, made as many as sixteen copies of this masterpiece. Of those completed by the son none are as whimsically complex as the original. This is always the case in literature, art, and music. The original is the best.

Here I provide an example of one proverb in the painting identified as number 3 in the monograph, *The Art of Mixing Metaphors*, by folklorists Alan Dundes and Claudia A. Stibbe, a superb duo. Their research was first presented at the Finnish Academy of Science and Letters in December 1980 and published by the *Academia Scientiarum Fennica* in 1981.

The depiction of the proverb shows a particularly unhandsome man with his hands close to his face. Hidden in shadows, he sits just inside a window of a tall house. His face is lean, his arms and hands equally lean; he appears undernourished and ready for the knife, as a knife does hang outside the window. For Dundes and Stibbe, the image "connotes overlooking something on purpose. One is willing to let a fault go unpunished." Some additional commentary concludes, "Since Bruegel's figure seems to be looking through his fingers, he presumably can take adversity in stride." These observations alone may not convince the average reader, but the erudite arguments of the two scholars march onward with observations that do convince; trust me, they are treating proverb number 3 with the seriousness of forensic specialists in a crime lab. They further suggest that the hand near the face may indicate that the figure is thumbing his nose at the world. I will not argue against this interpretation, but I put my foot down on another scholar's reading (referenced by Dundes and Stibbe) of the nose—a long, pointed snout—as a symbolic phallus. This scholar loses me there. In all my comings and goings in locker rooms, I have never seen a penis resembling a nose. The penis, like human sexuality in general, swings this way and that way. On second thought, the penis, like the nose, does occasionally poke into other people's business. Is that what the scholar means?

How I enjoy this card from Professor Mieder. How I wish I could sit before an Amsterdam canal, beer in hand, the shadows raking across those ancient buildings like a sundial. I could assemble, at my own sweet will, my own illustrations of proverbs.

Although that possibility seems out of reach, there's something I can do. Here I describe my volunteer work as the chief—and only—volunteer gardener at the Richmond Museum of History. *This* Richmond is in California. The museum, located in the ominously named Iron Triangle, is known for murder, drugs, rap of the foulest kind, cars that race maniacally, and a tsunami of sofas and refrigerators on the curb. Also, kindness that surprises. I'm always greeted politely and have never felt in danger, even when visiting a street memorial marking where a young man was gunned down. The candles at the memorial were nearly spent; a small, amber-colored whiskey bottle was empty; balloons, like used condoms, hung on a nearby fence.

On the west side of the Richmond Museum of History is a recycling center. While I garden, I can look up to see recyclers pushing shopping carts, pulling up in cars and trucks, or riding on bicycles, toting plastic bags as big as bears. I'm thinking of how the Dutch ships must have filled the harbors, how they came and went hauling cargo. The poor of Richmond, the down and out, the humanly complicated, have their own cargo. The crushing of cans and the breaking of bottles provides background music for their trade.

As the recyclers come and go, there are brief greetings among them—a cigarette is shared, a cellphone borrowed, change is made—and laughter and good-natured hollering. This is commotion at street level. If all the recyclers could gather for a moment into one pictorial herd, they would resemble the people in *Netherlandish Proverbs*, each with a proverb marking the story of their lives. Do I speak harshly? No. These citizens deserve close study. A gathering of university academics at a roundtable discussion could likewise embody their own telltale proverbs, each with their own folly, each with his or her own nose casting a shadow over their laptop computers.

I bring up these recyclers only because I see them twice a week; plus, as a poet, I recognize lives worth turning over in my mind. My time at the museum has involved me in chance meetings, such as helping to push cars that won't start. Taking an ill dog to the vet. Burying kittens alongside their mother. Buying medicine for a sick baby. Translating an English document for a Spanish-speaking domestic worker. Watching a street brawl between two young women, one of whom was topless at the bloody end.

Not far from the recycling center stands the Mission Rescue Center, a lifeline for those in need. Often, I see people walking down the street with loaves of day-old bread or pink boxes of stale pastry. More than once, a Chinese immigrant woman has offered me some of her food. She's country, totally country. I'll see her coming dressed in paisley pants and a striped blouse. I'll put my shovel aside and take off my gloves. She knows no

English, but she knows the meaning of the shovel in my hand. Proverbs must undoubtedly live inside her. In her heart, she must think, *This is a worker, this is someone with dirt under his fingernails.* She has no idea that I'm a volunteer with a sense of duty. She'll offer me a loaf or open a box and show me the doughnuts. Pieter Bruegel the Elder would have called her gesture the bread of life.

ABOUT
THE AUTHOR

GARY SOTO

GARY SOTO is a poet, essayist, playwright, author
of children's books, and, in this one-time effort, an influencer.
His books include *The Elements of San Joaquin, Living Up
the Street, Summer Life, Buried Onions, The Afterlife,* and
New and Selected Poems, a finalist for both the National Book
Award and *The Los Angeles Times* Book Award.
He is the author of "Oranges," one of the most
anthologized poems in contemporary literature.
He lives in Berkeley, California.

LIMBERLOST PRESS

www.limberlostpress.com

Dedicated to publishing finely printed books of poetry, fiction and non-fiction by both established and emerging writers.

Limberlost Press also publishes the

LIMBERLOST
REVIEW
A LITERARY JOURNAL OF THE MOUNTAIN WEST

The Limberlost Review *is a literary annual that features some of the best artwork and writing from the Mountain West and beyond, including poetry, fiction, memoir, essays, interviews, and re-readings, commentary about books we come back to again.*

For all editions (2019 through 2026) please visit:
www.limberlostpress.com

COLOPHON

This book is typeset in two fonts:
ITC Americana and **Goudy Old Style**.

Americana was designed by Richard "Dick" Isbell,
legendary graphic designer and type designer from
Detroit, Michigan. Isbell originally created the font in 1965
for the giant American newspaper and book company, Linotype.
It was chosen as the official U.S. Bicentennial typeface in 1976.
A few years later, Isbell and Jerry Campbell, a fellow type designer
and calligrapher from Detroit, modernized the font, reshaping it
to have thicker and thinner strokes for capitals and lower-cases.
It became widely used for headlines. Here, it is used for titling.
Isbell and Campbell also collaborated on the *Isbell* typeface.

The body copy for *Books as Drinking Buddies* is set in
an old-style serif typeface, **Goudy Old Style**. It was designed in
1915 by the American typographer, printer, and master designer
Frederic W. Goudy. He created the typeface on behalf of the
American TypeFounders (ATF), which was comprised of more
than 20 type foundries that merged to become the central hub
of type production in the U.S. during that period of time.
Goudy was a traditionalist who revered 16th-century Italian
book design and printing. Although he based his work on
typographic masters such as Nicholas Jenson (1420–1480),
Claude Garamond (1510–1561), William Caslon (1692-1766),
and Giambattista Bodoni (1740–1813), Goudy added his own
distinctive calligraphic elements. His namesake typeface became
a classic in American books and newspapers, known for
easy-to-read body copy, diamond-shaped periods and jots,
and graceful ligatures. Italic **Goudy Old Style** is easily recognized
by its ornamental letterforms. The font's shorter x-height often
challenges typographers and book designers to manually adjust
point sizes to make Roman and italic forms appear the same size.

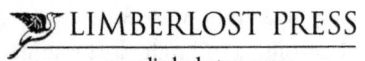
www.limberlostpress.com